BENDING TIME

A Collection of Short Stories

by

Stephen Minot

For the Louds Island
Library with thanks
for many happy
visits with
many of you

Stephen Minot

THE PERMANENT PRESS
Sag Harbor, NY 11963

Aug. '02

Library of Congress Catologing-in-Publication Data

Minot, Stephen.
    Bending Time/by Stephen Minot
        p.   cm.
    ISBN 1-877946-96-6
    I. Title.
PS3563.I475B46   1997
813'.54--dc20   96-36744
                                        CIP

First edition—September, 1997.

THE PERMANENT PRESS
Noyac Road
Sag Harbor, NY 11963

For Ginny

with love

To be on
time
in Time
took time.
For timing,
time and again,
depended on
elements
other
than men.

Angela Lorenz, from her
artist's book, *Librex Solaris*

Part I:
Bending Time and Memory

Part II:
Time in Exile

Part III:
Time in the American City

Part I

Time and Memory

A PASSION FOR HISTORY

Picture: On the shore where the river joins the sea, a lobsterman's boathouse-home, gray-shingled and trim, morning dew drifting in vapor from the roof, a column of smoke rising from the chimney, flower boxes with petunias. It's enough to turn the stomach.

He is not naive. He will not be trapped by sentimentality. He will not be seduced by those Currier-and-Ives virtues—thrift, honesty, piety, and hard work. These are slogans devised by those who control the means of production—the rich, the landholders, and the factory owners. There is no beauty in poverty.

Picture: On the ledge next to the lobsterman's home stands a couple. She wears a dress only a country girl would buy. Tall, long-boned, graceful, she would be beautiful if she had any notion of style. Beauty is there, hidden.

He has rumpled white pants and a blue polo shirt, the costume of a man consciously trying to be informal but not quite succeeding. He is older than she. But they are not father and daughter or brother and sister. As they look out on the glisten of the river that blends into the sea beyond, his right hand rests ever so gently on her right buttock.

They are mismatched, these two. It is more than her mail-order dress and his rumpled elegance, though that is part of it. There is some deeper aberration here. Like a parent, he can sense something wrong without being able to describe it. But he is not the man's parent. He is the man himself.

It is Kraft himself who is standing there. The woman beside him is Thea. The cottage where she lives is to their left. He is conscious now where his right hand is and can, in fact, feel the warmth of her body.

This kind of thing has been happening to Kraft lately.

He can't be sure whether some microcircuit in his brain is loose, blacking out certain periods of time, allowing him to stand on a bank *planning* to take a walk with someone and then skipping ahead to the actual event, or whether it works the other way around—being in the middle of an experience and suddenly viewing it from a distance, with historical perspective, as it were.

"Brooding?" she asks.

"Me? No. I don't brood. That's an indulgence. Thinking, maybe. Sorry. I was just thinking."

"Perhaps you miss teaching. Miss students and all that."

"No, not in the least. I'm not that kind of teacher, you know. A course here, a lecture series there. Not regular teaching. Not in my field."

He always downplays his university connections, he being a social historian, not a theoretician. He deals with reality, not speculation. A true radical, he disdains the trendy factions of his colleagues with all their jargon. He prefers to think of himself as a scholar in the true sense, a writer and lover of the past rather than a professor who holds a prestigious chair. Back home he would rather be known for his many articles on the lives of common people and for his recent volume on the radical movement in America.

But Thea, his lovely Thea, has read nothing, knows nothing about the outside world. She has never heard of him. He is for her just what he tells her about himself. She has lived her entire life here in rural Nova Scotia, his vacation retreat. Nova Scotia, a perfect time capsule, insulated against the realities of the twentieth century.

"I'd love to learn history," she says.

"Never mind that," he says. "You've got history in you. That's enough."

"But you teach, don't you? Teach history?"

"I don't teach history. I teach about people. Common folk. How they live. If you know how one person lives, you know a whole period. Not armies and national policy —just people. Do you understand?"

"Of course," she says, taking half a step back and turning just slightly to the right as if to search the treetops, checking to see if an osprey nest has been built during the night, and incidentally, innocently, pressing ever so gently against the palm of his hand with the curve of her bottom.

Picture: On the smooth, gray ledge that forms the bank of the Worwich River at the point where it flows into the sea, a man in white pants embraces a long, limber girl, kissing her, and is now beginning to undo the first of one hundred and two tiny, cloth-covered buttons that run down the back of her dress, she laughing, the sound drifting up like a loon's call. From this height one can see not only the little boathouse-home but the marshy estuaries formed by the meeting of river and sea, and farther, on the sea side, a great, gray-shingled rectangle of a house surrounded by tall grass, ledge outcroppings, and a scattering of overturned tombstones.

This large rectangle is the house Kraft has bought for himself and his family as a summer home—house and barn and outhouse and woodsheds and 953 acres of land. This is what he has bought with the royalties from his book on the radical movement in America.

Like a mistress, the place is an embarrassment and a pleasure. He makes a point of keeping it out of the press. His name is still mentioned in the press from time to time as "the one-time guru of radicals," but academic Marxists have written him off as an anachronism. He has no cult following, but he is read. His book is occasionally adopted for class use.

When interviewers press him, he refers to his property as his "rural retreat" or his "wilderness camp." In spite of this, a tediously strident Marxist historian has recently tried to write him off as one who bought up "a thousand-acre Nova Scotia dukedom." Kraft sees this as typical academic sniping that merely reflects the shameful level to which contemporary scholarship has sunk. Besides, the idiot has exaggerated by forty-seven acres.

His house up on the high land is in a permanent state of disrepair. He has not allowed one can of paint to be used inside or out. It is a weathered gray. There is no electricity, and water must be lifted bucketful by bucketful from an open well. The plaster was half gone when he bought it, so they removed the other half, leaving the horizontal laths as semipartitions between the rooms. It is, he reminds his family from time to time, their vista into the past.

But this spring there is no family. He came up alone in mid-April, leaving his wife and three children in New Haven by mutual agreement. He was to have two and a half absolutely clear months to complete the final draft of his most recent book, this one on the *liberal* tradition.

It is a perfect arrangement. No meetings to attend, no speeches to present, no teaching, no family to sap his energies. So of course he has done no writing.

There are times when he can't stand the clutter and filth of his own house—clutter, filth, and whispering deadlines. Those are the times when he comes here to the neat little boathouse-home on the river, the little Currier-and-Ives home Thea shares with her father.

Right now he is walking beside Thea, walking back to that perfect little place, his arm around her and hers around him. Seven of the one hundred and two tiny cloth-covered buttons down her back are undone. Ninety-five to go.

Kraft is not entirely certain that this is right. His wife, a sure and competent woman with a law degree and a practice of her own, would consider this a serious malady. Worse than the flu. On a par with income-tax evasion. And of course she would be right.

With these thoughts passing through his mind he sees in the far distance, inland, just coming out of the woods and beginning to cross the rocky field, approaching the boathouse-home, old Mr. McKnight.

"Oh," Kraft says, noticing for the first time that the barrow which the old man pushes has a handcrafted wooden wheel. Involuntarily Kraft's mind provides a parenthetical notation. (*Hand-fashioned oak wheels disappeared from each county at the point when mail-order houses reached that district.*)

"Oh," Thea says, not hearing his unspoken observation. "It's Father."

Kraft likes the old man—his courtly, country way. But he has mixed feelings about delaying what he and Thea had been heading toward.

"Well," she says, "it makes no nevermind. He'll stay for a while and we'll talk. But then it'll be time for his scavenging."

Every day at low tide the old man scours the beaches for usable items—timbers, orange crates, even nails that can be pried out and ground smooth on the whetstone. (*Recycling was an economic necessity for the rural poor long before its adoption as a* cause célèbre *by twentieth-century liberals.*) Clearly old Mr. McKnight lives in the previous century.

"I don't mind," Kraft says. Actually he does and he doesn't mind. Both. But that is too complicated to explain. Even to himself. "I don't mind," he says again. They are on the front stoop—a simple porch with no roof. She sits in the big rocker and he is perched on a nail keg old Mr. McKnight has salvaged from the sea. It will be a while before the old man puts the wood in the shed and comes around to suggest a mug of tea. Nothing whatever moves rapidly in rural Nova Scotia. Especially time.

"I don't mind," Kraft says, thinking that the last time he said it to himself in his own head. "It's good talking with the old man. Just this morning I wrote in my journal, 'I hope I see old Mr. McKnight today. He is my link with the region. I like hearing his voice. I learn a lot from him.'"

"Are you perhaps spending too much time with that journal of yours?" It is exactly the question his wife asked by letter the week before. Unsettling.

"I've kept that going ever since I was ten. I'm not going to stop now." He is, though, spending too much time writing in his journal and she knows it just as clearly as he does, so it is essential that he defend himself. "It's an act of survival, writing that journal."

"Survival?"

"Did you know that shipwrecked sailors rowing a

lifeboat must keep their eyes on their own wake? Otherwise they would turn in great circles. Did you know that?" She shakes her head. "I wrote about that last week, as a matter of fact. 'It's a paradigm for social continuity and tradition,' I wrote. Journals also give the writer identity. 'Sheepherders,' I wrote, 'talk to themselves and address their members with obscene endearments to maintain their sense of humanity.'" Or, he wonders, did he write "sanity"? "Well, I mean, here I am living in an ark of a house up there without electricity or running water miles from anywhere, adrift for two months with only a rough draft and a clutter of notes to work with and a publisher's deadline for navigation. Did you know that mermaids are an optical illusion caused by solitude and malnutrition?"

"I didn't know you believed in mermaids."

"I don't. You don't have to believe in them to know that they exist. I've got an entry about that too."

"Those entries," she says, shaking her head. He notices that she is shelling lima beans. Where did they come from? "You spend too much time with them," she says.

"It's just a trail of where my thoughts have been."

She shrugs. She is no lawyer and never argues. She makes commentary on his thoughts, but she never presses her point. "All that looking back," she says gently. "It'll turn you to salt." She smiles and a loon laughs. Either that or a loon smiles and she laughs. "Time to put the kettle on," she says. "He'll be coming in and wanting his tea right soon. Come sit with me while I fix up."

Picture in sepia: A woman stands by the soapstone sink, her hand on the pump. There is little light in the room because the windows are small. (*Large windows were avoided not only because of expense but because of a strong sense of nocturnal dangers. Except in cities, police protection was practically unknown.*) There is no view of the river or the sea.

The kitchen walls are made of the narrow tongue-and-groove boarding, a poor man's substitute for plaster. Open shelves rather than cupboards—the price of a hinge saved.

Kitchen table bare pine, unvarnished, scrubbed with salt—
to be replaced in the 1920s with white enamel. Kraft can
glance at a photograph of an American kitchen and date it
within a decade and can lecture without notes on its impact
on the status of women, the institution of marriage, and the
hierarchy within the family. Here in Worwich he has found
a lost valley. Time has moved on like a great flock of geese,
leaving a strange silence and sepia prints.

"He's been cutting wood," Thea says, taking the cast-
iron teakettle from the range and adding water to it from the
kitchen pump. Kraft's mind flashes a notation. (*The shift
from the heavy cast-iron kettle to the aluminum type was as
significant for women as the replacement of the wood range
by gas.*) "I imagine on your land."

"He's welcome to it. I've got enough problems without
clearing my own woodlots." He has a quick vision of his
study, the upper room in the big house on the bluff, his
papers scattered about like leaves after a storm. His manu-
script, the one on the American liberal movement, in cluttered piles; and in addition to his own journals there are his
father's journals, which he has foolishly brought. One more
distraction. One more bit of clutter. So if old Mr.
McKnight wants to poach, wants to clear land, he is welcome to it. Perhaps Kraft can persuade the old man to steal
unfinished manuscripts as well.

Simplicity. Order. He looks at Thea there at the sink.
She is both. Her cottage, her life is harmony. His own place
is a shambles. How can a man, he wonders, pick a summer
home so far from the complexities of contemporary society,
so painstakingly distant, and work so hard to keep the place
unimproved, simple, true to Thoreau, and still end up with
such an enormous rubbish heap in his own study?

The kettle has come to a boil. Thea measures loose tea
into a crockery pot and fills it with boiling water. She carefully arranges three mugs, spoons, and cloth napkins. He
feels a great wave of envy for her neat and orderly life, a
passionate and agonized longing that he mistakes for
healthy sexual desire.

"It is madness to romanticize nineteenth-century rural life," he has written in his journal only that morning. "Even a cursory examination of the McKnight family reveals a history of backbreaking work, sickness, and early death."

He silently recites his observation verbatim, cursed with total recall. No, blessed. Without some kind of historical sense of reality, this recent affair with Thea will turn into a nightmare of complications.

There is nothing to envy in Thea's life, he tells himself, and the affair is only a passing sexual fancy, a mildly comic sample of male menopause.

The evidence of brutish living is all around him, after all. Abandoned houses, cellar holes where families were burned out in midwinter, private cemetery plots grown over with chokecherry, no one left to tend them. One such is right on the rocky scrub grass he calls his front lawn. McKnights. Half of them children. A family shattered by the brutality of what they had hoped would be their New Scotland.

They came to the New World looking for the good life, and they hung on for more than two hundred years. But now as a clan they are broken and scattered, beaten by isolation, by madness, by sudden death, the younger ones fleeing to Montreal, to Toronto, to the States, the survivors selling the last remaining house and most of the land to this American historian and his family, who come north as summer residents, looking for the good life.

"Find it?" she asks.

"What?"

"Find it?" For an instant he believes she has a witch's ability to read minds. *Statements made about witches in the eighteenth century closely resemble fantasies of present-day patients diagnosed as paranoid; thus our clinical definition of mental illness depends from the outset on our current view of reality.*) But she has simply asked him for a pitcher of milk she has left on the windowsill to keep cool.

He sees it, hands it to her. She smiles. "If you don't want him cutting your wood," she says, "you should tell him."

Kraft shakes his head. "I'll never get around to clearing up those woodlots," he says. "There was a time when all the fixing up around the place went well. We really got a lot done. The boys and me working outside clearing fields and cutting back chokecherry. Good, honest work. And Tammy and my daughter working inside, making the place livable. Like a bunch of colonists. But then. . ."

His voice fades out. Why tell her all that? The second and the third summer—complaints from the children about the isolation; excuses to avoid the work; wry jokes about the lack of plumbing, the lack of electricity, the enforced intimacy; wisecracks growing sharper, less funny each summer. He finds this embarrassing. It is not the way he likes to think of his family. There is no need to share this with Thea.

She has finished the dishes and dries her hands on the roller towel, looking at him. Just the touch of a smile.

"They don't understand," she says. He wonders whether he has just voiced some of his disappointments or whether, again, she is reading his mind. "They don't understand, but I do."

"I don't know what I'd do without you," he says. Actually, he does know. It is unutterable. Everything would fall to pieces without her around to listen, to be his lover. It is not just sexual; it is human contact. He depends on both her and her father. Their presence. Both of them.

And there, suddenly, is old Mr. McKnight. He is standing at the kitchen door. Gray-bearded but with no mustache —a tintype. No smile but not unfriendly. (*It is a significant comment on the impact of the Industrial Revolution that from the introduction of the camera in the mid-nineteenth century until after the First World War it was not customary to smile when having one's picture taken.*) Old Mr. McKnight gives just the ghost of a nod of recognition and extends his hand in an Old World handshake.

"I couldn't seem to get any work done this morning," Kraft says. He doesn't want to seem like a summer resident.

"All that work with your head," Mr. McKnight says. "It can't be good."

"Right."

"Come look at this," the old man says. Kraft follows him into the workroom, where there is a skeleton of ribs fashioned to a backbone. It is the beginnings of a rowboat upside down, raised on two sawhorses. Mr. McKnight builds one a year, shaping the oak ribs in a crude boiler out back.

"Here," Mr. McKnight says, seizing Kraft's wrist. The old man's fingers are armored, rough plates joined. He takes Kraft's hand as if it were a plane and slides the palm along the oak keel. Kraft winces, expecting splinters from any unpainted surface. But of course it is perfectly sanded. Needlessly sanded.

"A filly's ass," the old man says.

"She's beautiful," Kraft says. "Like everything of yours."

"Ha!" Mr. McKnight smiles for the first time. The two men share their chauvinistic joke like a brotherhood—the younger one uneasily. "Time for a mug of tea," the odd one says just loud enough for it to become an order for Thea. "Tide's not about to wait for me or you."

Kraft nods, thinking: When the tide's out for you it will be high for Thea and me. He smiles to himself but Mr. McKnight casts a quick questioning look. Does the old man read thoughts too?

The three mugs have already been filled. Thea gestures to the table and remains standing until her father sits down. (*Informal eating was considered bad taste well into the 1920s and still is frowned on in rural Ireland and Scotland. The eating of food even under picnic circumstances was invested with ritual significance and required sitting correctly at a table.*)

"That skiff," old Mr. McKnight says, "is as fine as you can find here to Boston." (*Boston became a Nova Scotian term for all of New England by the 1780s*). "Not one bit of metal in her, you know. No nails. All pegged. Even the cleat is cedar heart. Hard as brass and it won't tarnish." He nods to himself in full agreement with himself. "Gives pleasure twice, it does—once in the building and again in the owning."

"In Halifax," Thea says, "they make them out of ply-wood."

They all three smile. "Imagine that," the old man says. Kraft does not mention fiberglass. For the McKnights it doesn't exist yet. "Halifax skiffs are nailed too. Full of nails. Rust out on you sooner or later. Ten, fifteen years they'll rust out on you. Drown you sooner or later. Like putting a metal wheel on a barrow. Takes me a month to shape a wooden wheel. Eight pieces glued and pegged. It's work, but it'll last a lifetime. Two, with luck. Same for lobster traps. Pegged and laced. You can't find a better trap."

Kraft nods, letting the old man continue, though he knows that in the States they are using a plastic lobster trap that is in every way superior. Ugly and indestructible as the aluminum beer can. "I build the best traps around here," the old man says. "The very best." They all nod, a part of the ritual. "Well, can't sit here all day. Tide's calling me," he says and abruptly he is gone. Quick as that.

And now, oddly, when the two of them are free, Kraft is hesitant. The room seems small, airless. Enclosing. Warily he looks to the window, to the door. He hears again the old man's proclamation—"I build the best traps."

He looks at her sitting there opposite him. For an instant she is in sepia again, posed there, a tall woman, high cheekbones. She is an image that would startle young readers browsing through an old photo album. "Who was that?" —the patronizing surprise of moderns who cannot imagine passion cloaked in formality. A sepia print. Colorless. How does such a lovely person stand a colorless life? How does she exist?

"What's wrong?" she asks. "You're having dark thoughts again."

"You're the one who should be having dark thoughts," he says.

"Why?"

"Cooped up here, trapped."

"I'm not trapped."

"With nothing to read."

"I'm not much for reading."

"No profession."

"I keep the place neat. I mend. Grow things."

"The monotony—it must be suffocating. I should think the isolation would drive you crazy."

"I'm not alone now."

"Now." She has no conception of future time. "Now." He stands up. He needs motion. "You know, don't you, that Tammy is coming up in ten days. Tammy and the children. And the dog. The whole bit. Did you forget that?"

"That's in a week. Now is now."

She floats in an eternal present. He can't imagine how that would be. He feels rage and envy. For him the present is the peak of a slippery hummock; he is forever sliding down one side or the other—either counting the days to something out there ahead of him or slithering back into the past.

He is standing behind her, his hands on her shoulders. She reaches up and takes both his hands and draws them down and around to her breasts. There is only the cotton fabric between his palms and the softness of her flesh. He feels her nipples. He stops thinking for an instant about past and future. I am holding the present in my hands, he thinks.

He is undoing the buttons down the back of her dress. She has leaned her head back so that it is against him, rocking gently.

"You're right," he says softly in her ear. "I'm not even going to think about Tammy."

Mistake. Mistake. The very word *Tammy* jars the mood, breaks his hold on the present. What is he doing? Somehow the action goes on, but he has floated up. The overview, the damned overview.

Picture: A man embraces a woman in an old-fashioned kitchen, her dress is loosened at the back, is down over one shoulder. The man is not at ease; he is harried by his passion, planning the next move, thinking ahead. He leads her up the stairs and into a simple, unadorned room: walls of vertical boarding, varnished dark. An iron bed, a rocking chair, a bureau with a wavy mirror attached, and a commode on which stands a kerosene lamp and a wash basin. Two books, a Bible and a copy of *Pilgrim's Progress*, both old. Perfect neatness. Perfect order.

Ninety-five tiny buttons open in a ripple and she stands bare-breasted in her petticoat. She shakes her hair down and it is long. Her petticoat slips to the floor at her feet. He has seen this image somewhere before, standing this way in the palm of an enormous seashell. But this is no time for art. She is with him on the bed. Her skin radiates warmth.

"Fast," he says. "Quickly." He is on an anxious schedule, racing to meet a sudden departure. The bed cries out like a flock of frantic gulls.

Then silence. Perfect silence.

That, one might imagine, was the climax of the day for him. But it was only the first of two. The second came after leaving.

He headed up the path toward his own house, not looking forward to returning, and he made the terrible mistake of looking back. A part of him knew that he shouldn't. But he had been living in the present tense and was careless. "Don't," he said to himself just as he turned, but it was too late.

There was the McKnight boathouse, the one he had just left, chimney smokeless, cracked, and leaning; the roof rotted through, sagging beams exposed, skeletal; windows all broken, flower boxes gone, wrenched off by the grinding ice of winter storms years ago. Dead. All dead and gone. All history.

THE SEAWALL

When Fern answered the phone it was Wesley. Poor Wesley was in the village and needed a ride home. It had been a miserable day. The air conditioner on the train was broken, there was no ice for drinks, and when he finally arrived his car battery was dead and it was going to be hours before they could get someone over to start it so someone should come down and pick him up. Right away.

"That's kind of a problem."

"Damn right it's a problem."

"I mean no one's here."

"You're there."

"Yuh, but. . ."

"Look, it was a hundred and ten in the club car and I'm stuck here with a dead car. Take Gwenda's. Key's over the visor."

Fern closed her eyes for a moment, seeing Wesley standing there in the phone booth outside the station, his white seersucker suit all wrinkled, one hand gripping the receiver and the other probably holding an Amtrak gin-and-tonic without ice, his enormous bulk dripping like a walrus stranded far from the sea. Wesley had been her stepfather for over a year, and just because she was so tall he refused to believe she was only fifteen and didn't have a license.

"Wesley, I don't have a license yet. Remember?"

"Well, get someone else then. Anyone. I don't care."

Fern stood there with the phone humming. He'd hung up. Not really angry, just gruff. That was his way. He probably got used to it at work. He was some kind of lawyer whose name kept appearing in the papers. His doctor had told him to retire, but Wesley had a very low opinion of doctors. As a compromise, he took the last train to Boston in the morning and the first one back. It was a big mistake to mention the word *retirement* when he was around.

He was full of complaints about the people who worked for him, but they probably made him feel like a king in there. Fern pictured harried secretaries and earnest young lawyers in three-piece suits all jumping whenever he gave orders. He probably got a kick out of all that attention and having people do things his way, but it sure got a little tiresome at home.

"Gwenda!" she called. But she knew her mother wasn't home. This was her tennis day. Fern hung up the phone and looked out across the patio to the bay. The water was flat. The glare made her squint. Yes, poor Wesley would indeed expire if she didn't get someone down there.

She dialed Bibbo's number and let it ring for a long time. Bibbo was her father and lived with his new wife, Betty, in the next house, just down the beach. Like all the homes along that section, it had once been a summer place. But now it was for year-round. It was wonderful, everyone said, that Fern could live with her mother and Wesley or over with Bibbo and Betty, or even up the hill with Bibbo's mother, Mumsie. Fern had her choice, free to move about not by any legal arrangement but just as she wished. It was, Gwenda often said, very civilized.

Bibbo wasn't home, of course. Bibbo worked long hours redesigning and restoring historic homes and usually took the very last train from Boston. But surprisingly Betty wasn't there either. No one knew what Betty did with her time.

"Great," Fern muttered. "Just great."

She thought of going up to her grandmother's; but no, Mumsie would be no help either. She used to have a car and a driver and that would have solved everything, but she had given both up because there wasn't as much money around as there used to be. The only other member of the family was Luke. He was Wesley's son. He lived in a tent next to the beach and never came into the house.

Fern left the house and walked along the seawall, enjoying the warmth of the concrete on her bare feet. Whenever she walked the wall she kept her eyes on the bay and the open sea beyond. Some days it was soothing, some days exciting and dangerous, but always it was open and inviting. She wished she could sail right out into it and not stop, just keep on sailing toward the horizon, come what may.

"Hey Luke!"

He was not in his tent but was sitting on the seawall with a can of beer. He'd spent most of the summer there, looking out to sea, nursing a can of beer. Sometimes he shot sea gulls from there with a revolver and ate them. Luke made everyone nervous.

"Hey Luke," she said, "you've got to help."

She knew at once she'd taken the wrong tack. It just didn't work to say "got to" to Luke. Sure enough, he grinned and shook his head. A great start.

"O.K., O.K., so you don't *have* to. But your father's down at the station and his car's got a dead battery or something. He's very hot."

"Dad's very hot?" Luke said, looking up at her. Somehow that struck him as funny. "*Real* hot?"

"You know what it's like in the village when there's no wind."

"Hot? Look, Sweet Pea, I could tell you about hot."

She nodded. *Hot* meant Vietnam or oil rigs in Texas or work boats in Louisiana. He never talked much about his experiences, but he kind of gave the impression that the family didn't know much about the outside world.

"I thought maybe you could pick him up. You could take Gwenda's car."

"You need a key to run those things."

"The key's over the visor."

"I don't feel much like it."

"Come on. Why not?"

"Why not? Let me count the ways, Sweet Pea." He offered her his warm beer, but she shook her head. "Let's put it this way, why *should* I?"

"Because there's going to be a big noise if you don't,

25

that's why. He'll have to wait for Bibbo to give him a ride and he he'll come home all pissed and blame Gwenda and she'll shout at him and no one will get any sleep, that's why."

"Shouting? I can barely hear them from here. Let go, kid, they're all grown up. How come he doesn't take a cab?"

"There's only one and Wesley won't speak to him. You weren't here then, but last winter he did take the cab and the guy said something nasty about the tip and—well, you know how Wesley is at the end of the day—he bellowed at the driver and then at us all evening. It was a real show. He wouldn't call them if they had the last car on earth."

Luke leaned back on his elbows and laughed. She could see his Adam's apple pulsing. The skin there wasn't tanned because of his beard, and it looked strangely naked.

He wore dirty white pants and no shirt and his skin everywhere but under his beard was bronzy like a castaway. She wondered if Gauguin had looked like that. But this was crazy—she was forgetting all about Wesley down at the depot.

"Look," she said, "he's *your* father."

He stopped laughing. "You think? Listen, Sweet Pea, I'm thirty-five this summer and no one my age has a father."

So Luke didn't go to pick up his father, and Fern went out on the sailfish so she wouldn't hear the phone, paddling on her stomach for lack of wind. There was a kind of gull that stayed at sea all its life. That would really be something. Trouble was, she'd get hungry. She'd have to come back for that. Besides, they'd call her back.

Wesley had a bullhorn that carried for miles.

* * *

"Fern dear, it's time you kept track of things." Gwenda, just back from the club and still in her whites, was flipping through Fern's dresses, trying to decide which Fern should wear. "I mean, you're not a child any more. You're almost as tall as me, right? When you're a kid, you just tag along and no one expects you to remember where we're going or when. But you must be—what, fifteen? Fifteen. Time you kept a social calendar. Your father's been planning this wing-ding for weeks. At the dock. With the bar on the *Victoria.* A little cutesie, if you ask me, but you know Dad."

"He's not *your* dad, Gwenda."

"Honey, don't you think this first-name business is kind of a—what, affectation? I mean he *is* your father, and you may not be thrilled but I *am* your mother and most people don't mind using words like *mother* and *father.* Jesus, I call Bibbo's mother *Mumsie* as you well know, and no one thinks that's strange."

"I do."

"Don't get flip." She held up one of Fern's dresses, considered it seriously, but then shook her head. "It's not that I think highly of motherhood, I'm only concerned with your using the language properly. With everything else crumbling, we might as well hang on to the language. Say, how about this little print thing?"

"You mean 'dress'?"

Gwenda sat down on the bed, hauled out another cigarette and lit it. "Fern baby, I do *not* need a lot of smart talk. I really don't. You're still a kid, you know. Don't start sounding like a grownup."

"Sorry."

"Things have not gone well today. Wesley's car broke down. . . ."

"I know. He called."

". . .right in the village. Poor Wesley, you know how he loves that machine. And then it goes and fails him. He had to wait there until Bibbo came in on the 6:02—for over an hour! And Bibbo's not always the most sensitive type as you well know and somehow the thought of Wesley sitting there without a drink for an hour in that cruddy little station —well, it made your father start laughing and he couldn't stop which was not a good idea because Wesley has a short

27

fuse as you well know and if he hadn't been absolutely played out with heat prostration he would have flattened your father. With perfect justification, I might add. Fortunately Wes somehow held his temper—I mean, he *did* need that ride—but your dear father couldn't stop razzing him all the way back. You know how he is. So Wesley ended up telling your father that we weren't going over there tonight, any of us, and, Jesus, you know what it's going to be like around here if we don't show up at this late date. Betty would not handle it well. You know how I love her. She's a—what, gem? Yes, really a gem. Of sorts. But she's Southern."

"Tennessee."

"That's South, believe me. They're *more* Southern because they're not *really* Southern, if you know what I mean. She takes things very seriously—in a flighty sort of way. So I'm in an awkward spot. I mean, we surely don't need another dreary little feud spoiling the peace and quiet of the summer and frankly, Fern, frankly, I just can't stand . . .I just can't stand having you get sulky just when I need you."

She inhaled very deeply, held it the way Fern's older cousins smoked dope, and then blew it out. Her eyes were welling up and Fern decided to be really nice.

"You pick out something for me," she said. "Whichever one you want."

* * *

It seemed odd to Fern at first that she and Gwenda should both be getting dressed for the party if Wesley had decided flatly that none of them would go. But then she realized that she was expected to straighten things out with him. So she put on the long Indian print skirt her mother finally picked out and a white blouse and pulled her hair back tight with a barrette. Wesley took a dim view of loose hair.

Wesley was on the patio out front. He was still in his rumpled seersucker, his tie loosened, top button undone.

Although he was facing the sea, he was not looking at it. He was holding his martini in both hands, studying its depths. Fern was relieved that the glass was full. Since he had been home a good twenty minutes, this would be his second drink, which would make things somewhat easier. She sat down opposite him, close enough to rest her hand on his knee.

"One more year and I'll have my license," she said.

He shrugged without looking at her. She wondered if maybe he had sunk into one of his sulks. That would be a problem because once he was dug in he wouldn't talk to anyone for hours. He'd just stare into his drink as if it were a crystal ball and everyone would have to tiptoe around him. But no, she could see that he was not sulking, he was building up a head of steam. His lips were quivering, forming words the way they did when he was rehearsing a speech. She could almost see phrases bubbling up to the surface. Finally he looked her straight in the eye.

"Can you imagine committing the integrity of a 100-year-old firm to a stockholders' class-action suit *pro bono*, mind you, with the promise of lengthy litigation involving successive appeals in three states and an outcome which is guaranteed, *guaranteed* to be a high dive into a wet sponge? Can you imagine it?"

"I sure can't."

"Of course you can't. Even you know what kind of risk is involved. Loring told me in no uncertain terms this would be a 28 percent time commitment and not even a contingency fee for the first three years so of course we got a negative vote from the advisory board and a recommendation for arbitration but. . . ."

She kept nodding and studying his face. There was never any point in trying to follow these things. They were more like operas where the words don't count. His fleshy cheeks were getting red and also his neck, veins bulging, and beads of sweat on his brow, white hair getting all fuzzed up. He was really rather impressive once he got rolling and she could see how juries and judges would be held by him. Oh, he was sure into it now but it made him sweat terribly and she must remember to ask Gwenda if his heart was O.K. because that vein looked ugly and he seemed to have trouble getting his breath.

"So," he said, glaring at her, "what do *you* think?"

"They must be really crazy."

He threw his great bulk back in the chair and shouted, "Gwenda, Gwenda! This kid of yours is a thundering genius!"

But Gwenda was listening to "A Little Night Music" in the Jacuzzi. Fern leaned forward and placed her hands on his knees. "Hey, Wesley, how about putting on your blazer so we can go to Bibbo's party?"

* * *

The house that Bibbo and Betty had was the one in which Fern had grown up. It was older and a little shabbier than the one Mumsie bought for Gwenda after the divorce. But it was closer to the seawall and had a pier at which Bibbo could keep his schooner at dockside rather than out on a mooring.

The *Victoria* was really an extension of the house. People said she was a classic. She had a wooden hull painted black with varnished spars and brass fittings that had to be polished. She leaked a lot, but she was beautiful. Whenever they went cruising, people in port would row out just to stare and sometimes take photographs. Bibbo was very fond of her, but Betty was not. Everyone said that must be because she came from Tennessee. She didn't like parties either. She was a bit dumpy and said all those hors d'oeuvres were a temptation. She also didn't enjoy loud people. She said once, smiling, that northerners seemed to shriek a lot.

There were already a number of cars parked in the circle, but many people had walked. It was that kind of area. "Laid back and natural," Gwenda often said. As they entered the house they could see through the glass doors on the sea side, across the lawn to the pier where everyone was. It was twilight and the guests looked ruddy and healthy in the glow of the setting sun and the Japanese lanterns strung between the masts.

Fern wanted to leave Gwenda and Wesley as quickly as possible and go on board. She liked to sit up on the forward hatch. Women with their spiky heels didn't dare leave the cockpit, so Fern could watch the party from the bow without having to make conversation. Gwenda was forever trying to get her to circulate more at parties, but Fern didn't see the sense of it. Boys her age were gawky, and college students backed off as soon as they heard how young she was. Gwenda said that with Fern's height all she needed now was to fill out a bit and that as soon as she had something to show she would attract boys like flies. Fern wasn't sure whether that was good or bad.

They were passing through the deserted living room when Betty appeared from nowhere, struggling with a large silver tea tray loaded with hors d'oeuvres. Betty was shorter than Gwenda and a bit heavier. No one could understand why Bibbo would go for someone like that. Fern figured it was because she did everything she could to make Bibbo happy. He wasn't used to that.

"Two of those dear local girls just didn't show up," Betty said, smiling bravely. "Can you imagine? Not so much as a note of apology! Oh Fern dear, would you?" Without waiting for an answer she handed Fern the tray. And turning to Wesley, "I'm so glad you all decided to come, I truly am."

"Why wouldn't I?" Wesley said.

Betty, flustered, tried to kiss Gwenda, which was a mistake because Gwenda hated to get smudges of lipstick on her and did her best just to touch the cheek of would-be kissers.

"So good to see you," Betty said.

"It's been hours," Gwenda said.

"Everyone's down by the pier."

"I was wondering."

"Maybe I'd better pass these around," Fern said. Anything to get the family split up and circulating before there was real trouble.

Passing a heavy tea tray heaped with pigs-in-blankets was not Fern's idea of fun. She wondered how long it had taken Betty and her one remaining hired girl to wrap each oyster in its blanket of bacon before baking. It was much too complicated for a large crowd, but as Gwenda said, it was Betty's nature to fuss a bit.

The tray was an enormous, ornate thing intended for an entire tea service and barely portable. The trouble was that she had to keep holding it while grownups who hadn't seen her since last summer asked the same set of questions—was she really Fern? How tall she'd grown! Was she in college now? No? Fern would have to explain that she went to boarding school in Connecticut and then they would ask which courses she liked. Luke was probably right. He said folks around there weren't all that bright and couldn't think of anything else to say.

Then there were those who didn't know her at all. The condo crowd, Bibbo called them. Often they assumed she was a maid. "Hey miss," the men would say. Sometimes she would feel a hand on her bottom and had to move fast.

Bibbo was in the cockpit talking with two women and helping the bartender mix drinks at the same time. He did it with a flourish and without measuring. People sometimes asked Fern how he stayed so young-looking and she was never sure how to respond. But they were right. He looked marvelous in his blue blazer and his white flannels—slim, trim, and tanned. He sure made other men seem stodgy.

She went over to him and he grinned, shaking his head in mock dismay at her being asked to perform as a maid. He relieved her of the tray, setting it on the gunwale, saying "Hey Fern, Lover-girl." He hugged her enthusiastically and, still holding her, finished a story he had been telling the two women behind Fern's back. "So there he was with Germany's finest example of automotive engineering—and it won't run!"

Everyone laughed except Fern. He let go of her. "Wesley," he said.

"I know. Look, anything you want me to do?"

"Everything's taken care of. Don't you worry your little head over a thing. Betty's a master at affairs like this. Her specialty. Has everything running like clockwork. How's my pal Wes getting along? Still simmering?"

"Hey, could you take it easy on him?" She tried to keep her tone light. "He's had a rough day."

"A rough day? The great legal eagle? Nothing wrong with him except his battery's run down." He winked at the two women and they laughed.

"Just don't razz him any more, O.K.?"

"Hey, we're pals. I gave him a ride, didn't I? And that's not all I've given him."

"Hey, Bibbo!"

"Just kidding." He turned back to the two women. "Really we're regular pals. After all, we've shared so much." The women shrieked with laughter, one of them telling Bibbo that he was *very* naughty, stepping back with fresh laughter, nudging the silver tea tray. It slipped noiselessly overboard. No one but Fern noticed. She looked over the side and saw the last of the pigs in blankets bobbing in the dark water.

"Look," Bibbo said, speaking to Fern but holding one of the women by the elbow to keep her from drifting off, "relax and have a good time. Find some guy and tell him you go to Barnard. That's what your Aunt Tillie did back when she was your age and no one can accuse her of not having had a good time in her day." Fern remembered visiting her Aunt Tillie in a hospital, but probably that had nothing to do with pretending she went to Barnard. "Don't be such a worrywart," Bibbo said. He gave one of his quick imitations of a worrywart nibbling a worryberry and made her giggle. "Oh, do me a favor, will you? Mumsie has a hard time at these things because she can't hear well. She's over there on the bench. . . ."

He gave Fern a little nudge as if they were playing Pin

the Tail on the Donkey and asked his two friends if they had heard about Wesley's altercation with the plumber. They shook their heads, grinning in anticipation. Fern wondered how she was going to keep Wesley out of range up on the dock. She'd have to get a drink to him before he came down. Maybe two just to be sure.

She asked the bartender for two gin-and-tonics—doubles with no lime (garbage, Wesley called it)—and tried to worm her way from the cockpit back up to the pier. She couldn't find him, though, so she went over to where she knew Mumsie would be, her hands growing numb with the two drinks.

The trouble with Mumsie was that she was too nice. She was forever inviting Fern to come up for a meal or tea and then suggesting that Fern move up there, live with her at least for the summer. She told Fern she could have friends in any time, but there weren't many people Fern's age around there. The only girls she knew were from boarding school and lived in Connecticut or Long Island or California. Besides, she couldn't imagine introducing anyone her age to all this.

"Fern dearest, you are a sight for sore eyes. Did you bring that for me? I hope it doesn't have gin in it. I'm just too fond of gin and always have been. No, I can see it doesn't. I don't touch anything alcoholic any more except late in the evening and then just for sleep or maybe before lunch and of course a dash of cognac in my tea to free the phlegm, but you don't have to worry about phlegm yet and if I were you I wouldn't touch alcohol until you're my age. I keep telling that father of yours that this family has a proclivity for sociability and he should watch out for too much of this sort of thing." She gestured to the party with her glass, spilling some of it. "You really should consider moving up the hill with me. Quieter there. And Lord knows there's room enough. We had seven children in that house—summers only, of course—plus plenty of staff, and I've watched them go off one by one. Servants included. They're all gone— except for your father, bless him. I'm afraid the place is a bit scruffy, but you'd make such a difference. Maybe you could mow the old croquet lawn if there isn't too much bull briar. Miss Klauss is a holy terror on the croquet lawn." Miss Klauss was Mumsie's nurse. She always wore a white starched uniform and had never been known to smile. Bibbo called her the Virgin Hun. "The three of us," Mumsie said, "could have our own little tournaments!"

* * *

Later that night Fern found herself walking Mumsie up the winding road to her house on the hill. She held one elbow and Miss Klauss, her uniform gleaming in the dark, held the other. Miss Klauss had an odd way of clearing her throat every minute or so. This little "ar-umpf" combined with her perpetual frown made everyone feel as if they were doing something wrong.

Most of the time Mumsie kept on a straight course, but occasionally she had to be nudged. Miss Klauss would shake Mumsie needlessly and Fern would say, "You're doing fine"—more to keep Miss Klauss from being so rough than as reassurance to Mumsie who had the hiccups and couldn't hear anyhow.

It seemed like a long way, Mumsie taking all those tiny steps, talking all the while about family members Fern could barely remember. Mumsie tended to mix up the generations a good deal, so it was not always possible to tell whether she was discussing the living or the dead. When they finally got to the house and were standing on the great veranda that overlooked the bay, Mumsie started in on the invitation again, but Fern was used to that. No, she would rather not stay and have a cup of Ovaltine; no, she didn't think she'd be able to come over first thing in the morning; no, she really was happy living where she was but, yes, maybe some summer she would stay with Mumsie and Miss Klauss, the three of them like a little family, and Miss Klauss would teach Fern how to play mah-jongg because that's what they did every evening as soon as the meal was over and it wasn't a game designed for just two people. Wouldn't that be lovely? Yes, that sounded like a wonderful summer.

Miss Klauss suddenly spoke for the first time that evening. She said to Mumsie: "Enough of that. You come along right now."

Mumsie clutched Fern's wrist, looking up at her with watery blue eyes.

* * *

As Fern made her way down the curving road toward Bibbo's party she realized that she was still carrying the remaining double gin-and-tonic with no fruit, and although it was warm and useless it reminded her that if Wesley and Bibbo got together at this hour there could be real trouble. It would help if Gwenda would get Wesley home early, but she was a real night person and while she never seemed drunk she sometimes forgot she was divorced from Bibbo. Wesley did not take kindly to evenings like that.

"Hey, Sweet Pea!" The voice came from the dark and made her jump.

"Luke?"

"Over here." Luke was sitting on the hood of someone's car. "You sure took your time."

"I was walking Mumsie. . . ."

"I know. They told me. I've been waiting."

"For what?"

"You."

"Why?"

"I'm taking off."

"At this hour?"

"Ever hear about taking off under a cloud?"

"You have an argument with Wesley?"

"Real heavy." He took the drink from her hand, drained it, and tossed the glass over someone's garden wall. "He's not the easiest father, you know."

"You told me people your age didn't have parents."

"Don't believe everything I say."

There was a pause. Fern could hear the distant sound of the party. It came to her like a steady wail. His leaving seemed inexplicable. But then she'd never understood why he'd come in the first place. It had been early spring when he arrived from nowhere and pitched that tent as far as he could from the house and still be on the property. Until then, Fern didn't even know she had a stepbrother. All summer she brought him food as if he'd been a stray cat. Sometimes when Wesley and Gwenda had guests Luke would squat at the edge of the patio for the evening, just out of sight. He kept hidden like a jungle cat and didn't do them any harm. But occasionally someone would spot him staring at them. Gwenda would explain that Luke was "between jobs" and trying to "find himself." Everyone was nice about it, but they tended to go home early. "My father hasn't discovered the pleasures of occasional indolence."

"I know. I told them you were writing a war novel."

Luke grinned. "I'll do that when peace breaks out."

"Luke, there's no trains at this hour. Or busses or anything."

"I'm taking Gwenda's car. Key's over the visor, I hear."

"He'll put you in jail. He really will."

"No he won't. You can't put your own son in jail, right?"

"You told me not to believe you."

He hopped down from the hood. "I'll leave it where they can pick it up in the morning. Hey, how about coming along? Head west. No sweat, we could be just buddies if you want. Old wartime buddies. Just head for the horizon. How about it?"

Fern took in a deep breath. Then she shook her head and reached up to kiss him. She wanted to give him a long, sophisticated kiss he'd really remember, but tears started running down her face and her nose stopped up so quickly she had to quit in order to breathe.

* * *

Hurrying back to the party, she hoped that she would find Wesley at that stage when he couldn't complete sentences, ending each with a kind of rumble. Most people took that to be anger ("What was Wesley so worked up over last night?") when in fact he was at his most pliable and would let Fern lead him away, lead him home again. With luck, she might include Gwenda too, keeping Gwenda from getting a second wind and teaming up with Bibbo, the two of them doing their soft-shoe routine together for old times' sake and singing "You Are My Sunshine" in harmony, which everyone loved but was also about the only event which could cause Betty to lose that smile of hers and lock herself in the bathroom for the whole of the next day with Bibbo saying to Fern, "Talk to her through the door, will you? Tell her nothing went on, nothing, will you?"

Fern started across the lawn toward the pier when she was intercepted by Betty coming the other way.

"Fern dear," she said with that ever-present smile, "wherever have you been? We need you." Fern wondered how to explain the missing tea tray, but Betty hadn't noticed. "Fern dear, I seem to have this headache and I know it's just terrible of me but I've got to get my beauty rest and I was wondering if you wouldn't like to stay over? I mean on the boat."

Normally Fern liked to sleep on board, but it was clear that the party wouldn't be breaking up for hours and someone always managed to throw up in the cabin. "Tonight?"

"Well, it would save you walking back." (Was she serious?) "And everyone's about to go."

"Maybe tomorrow."

"No, *tonight.*" No smile this time. Uh-oh. "Fern, I don't mean to burden you, but I'm asking you to stay on board. I mean I try, really I do. No one knows how hard I try. I made all those lovely things to eat and I talked to just about everyone here and I'm spending my afternoons at a tacky little YWCA doing aerobics every afternoon trying to lose weight until I ache all over, but no matter what I do that boat turns into—excuse my language—into a broth-el. So if you just stayed there, you see they. . ." She was clinging to Fern and swaying. Her perfume smelled of musty lilac. "It's not right, Fern, it's not moral—what your parents do with each other."

* * *

Back at the party, Fern still couldn't find Wesley. She hoped he hadn't left early because then he'd see Luke taking the car and that would make things complicated. But then she couldn't find Bibbo either, and she wondered if the two of them had gone off together. Bibbo had an odd way of pretending Wesley was his very best friend and walking along the beach with him, arm around his shoulder, sort of kidding him, giving him little pokes in the stomach and laughing until Wesley, who had his limits, finally punched him in the face. No one ever got seriously hurt, but it wasn't a good way to end a party.

Bibbo wasn't anywhere on the pier or in the cockpit. And no one was up forward on the deck. Where was Gwenda? Oh boy, the two of them off somewhere. The cabin! Just what Betty predicted. Was that really illegal?

She went down the companionway cautiously, figuring the best approach would be to cough and ask something stupid like whether Betty was there and then back out quickly enough so they wouldn't think she'd seen anything.

But the jolt wasn't what she expected. She stepped into a foot of black water. It was surprisingly cold. The cabin lights were dim, but she could make out the rear end of a man bent over in the head. Why would anyone kneel in all that water to throw up in the bowl?

"Bibbo, is that you? Are you all right?"

"Everything's just dandy."

She looked at the cushions and cracker boxes floating in the water and without thinking clearly said, "Did you know that there's a lot of water here?"

Bibbo snorted. "You noticed?" But when he pulled himself out of there, his white pants clinging to him, his shirt stained, he wasn't smiling. "Jesus, girl, where have you been? You wander off just when I need you. Someone's smashed the bowl here. Smashed it right down to the valve. Some goddamned loony. Get me something to plug it."

"Shouldn't we warn the others?"

"Keep your voice down. You want to ruin the party? Get me something to stuff in here. Every time I let go, it really spurts."

They were interrupted by a woman calling down from the companionway. "Wesley? Is that you?" It was Gwenda.

"Wesley's up at the bar getting sloshed."

"But I just saw him go down there."

"You what?" Bibbo ran for the companionway, stumbling through water. "That son of a bitch!"

"Water!" Gwenda shrieked. "Good God, we're sinking!"

* * *

So Fern didn't have to sleep on board that night. She found it impossible to plug the leak and the electric pumps wouldn't work, the batteries drained from the Chinese lanterns. She struggled with the hand pump, but there was no way she could keep the ship afloat. Bibbo and Wesley had one awful fight on the beach and neither of them saw that lovely schooner go down at the pier.

The crowd responded with late-night enthusiasm. After the initial shrieks of mock panic and cries of "women and children first," they stood on the pier, watching and chattering, cracking jokes. There was absolutely nothing that anyone could do. As the waters finally closed over the cabin with a kind of sucking noise, a great cheer went up. Fern closed her eyes tight and shouted, "Shut up! Shut up! *Shut up!*"

Running back along the seawall, she reached her

mother's house. It was dark and quiet. Then she continued to where Luke's tent was.

"Luke?"

There was no answer. He'd made it. He'd taken his sleeping bag and pack, but he'd left her the tent and an old army blanket neatly folded. Inside it there was a big candy bar. As she unwrapped it, she saw something scrawled on the back. "Sweet Pea" it said. She curled up in the blanket and munched the chocolate. The sound of the water lapping just the other side of the seawall and the taste of the chocolate were as sweet as anything that had come her way in a long time. How'd he know she'd be staying here anyhow?

A SOMETIMES MEMORY

Malvina Hodgson Boone sits alone at the end of the couch, watching. The room is full of relatives. They are drinking cider and eating potato salad. They are talking to each other in subdued tones the way Hodgsons often do. She watches, hands in her lap. No one is talking to her.

No one is talking to Malvina Hodgson, she says to herself. Malvina is sitting at the end of the couch, watching, and no one is speaking to her—none of her brothers or her sisters or her father. Aren't her sons here? No one is talking to Malvina Hodgson, but she isn't sorry for herself or bitter. She merely watches, putting faces and names together.

Malvina is forty-five and slightly overweight. At college she was a champion swimmer and played tennis with men. But over the years there was less and less chance to exercise. When she and her husband lived in Venezuela there were servants to do everything. That was the beginning of trouble. And of course the children. The boys. Where are the boys?

"Hello." A girl is looking down.

"Yes?"

"It's good having you here." The girl pauses. There is a tense look in her eyes like a child on stage who is unsure of her lines.

She's not a Hodgson. Young enough to be a second cousin or a niece, but she hasn't the build. Too slight. Narrow shoulders. Narrow hips. Poor girl will have a terrible time in childbirth. Strange that she should welcome me here, her not even a Hodgson. Probably has me confused. No wonder, with all these people.

"Why shouldn't I be here?" This without bitterness. "I'm one of the family."

The girl sits down beside Malvina. She is very serious.

She puts her hand on Malvina's shoulder. "Mom, are you. .
. ?" Her pretty little mouth remains open, groping for words.
"You have no cider. I'll get you some."

"No, no cider, thank you."

"I'll get you some."

She's a foolish little girl, Malvina thinks, watching her
skinny back turn this way and that, weaving her way
through the crowd, dodging clumps of adults and little knots
of children. And very awkward. Strange how awkward
these young ones are. No social ease. Not sure of who I
am. Not sure of what to say.

But she doesn't mind being left alone. It is a strain to
be taken for someone else.

Malvina Hodgson sits alone sipping cider. She has been
mistakenly taken for someone else by a young girl. The
young girl does not introduce herself because that is the
way they are these days. It is not rudeness. They simply
don't take names as seriously as we did. Particularly last
names. It's just the times, Dad. You've got to get used to
it. Why, young Byron came to visit with his girl and never
did mention her last name. To this day I don't know what
it is; and there's nothing really wrong with that, actually. Is
there? But it infuriates Father. Incivility, he calls it. Hates
incivility.

Malvina's father is Dr. Bertrand Hodgson. Everyone
knows him. He returned to this, the town of his birth, right
after medical school and served as its only obstetrician for
forty-two years. He watched the town grow from a coastal
farming village into a popular tourist area and didn't like the
change. Men with open shirts; women in pants. No end to
it. But loved by everyone. And why not? He has brought
most of them into the world. At his testimonial there were
fifty-two men and women there who owed their arrival to
him. And he remembered them all by name. Every one.
Them and the 560 who had moved away. More than six
hundred people. Most of them send Christmas cards every
year.

Dr. Bertrand Hodgson is a rock. People say that of him.

They mean he is very sure of everything. He's sure of everything because he's lived here all his life. All his life, Malvina says to herself, in this stuffy little town. You never got to know how other people think staying here, she tells him silently. You never got to know how *we* think. Spending all those hours at work. Evenings and weekends. Jumping up from meals to deliver more children. Leaving everything to Courtney. Making him boss his own brothers and sisters. No wonder Courtney resented it. Hated us. No wonder he was mean. You did it, Malvina says silently to her father with a shiver of rebellion. As soon as you bring children into the world you forget them. Forget us. You and your dedication.

No, that's not fair, Malvina. There isn't a soul in this town that doesn't love the man. She nods to herself, closing the conversation. There are some topics that are best left alone. Besides she's not to talk to herself that way. It isn't healthy.

She concentrates on the room. She's sitting at the end of a hard horsehair couch that makes her back ache. Echoes from childhood—both the couch and the ache. Mother never allowed them to lean against the back. It softens the spine, leaning back. And, to the left, that dark old bookcase with glass doors. The large family Bible and the smaller one for evening use. The Book of Common Prayer and the hymnal. But enough of that. She is not to indulge in self-pity. It's not healthy.

So many people! They can't all be Hodgsons. So many strange faces. Didn't there used to be a kerosene heater there? And the old pump organ between the windows? No loss, really, but somehow disturbing to see it gone. Perhaps they've removed it just to make room. Could that be Jay? No, he'd be older than that. Strange, but it *has* been twenty years. Perhaps more. All of us scattered so, flying apart just as soon as we could. And now drawn together again. So many here at the same time. All gathered for. . . ?

Malvina sits alone at the end of the horsehair couch wondering what the reunion is for. No one will tell her. No

one quite trusts her. Even this morning. Malvina rises with
the others and eats with the others like every day and then
Sally the pretty little nurse says, "Malvina, you'll be visiting
with your family today. How are you feeling?" Why is Sally
so solemn? Malvina feels a surge of elation. She hasn't been
allowed home in years. Why shouldn't she feel elated?

She looks up at a group talking close by and sees her
oldest brother, Courtney. Mean Courtney. It is hard to link
this distinguished older man with the Courtney of her memory—the boy with the shabby elbows and the nasty laugh,
the boy who bossed all five of them because he was older
and stronger. It was Courtney who assigned the chores
around the place and punished them when they forgot,
whipping them on the backs of their legs with an old length
of clothesline he kept in the barn. No, this man here looks
much more like her father in his prime. Strong and handsome. He pays no attention to her. Just as well.

"Malva! Hallelujah!"

"Yes?"

A plump, smiling man is standing in front of her. "Oh,
come on, now, I haven't changed a bit, right? Thin as ever
and glossy-haired." He pats his paunch and then runs both
hands across the hairless globe of his head, laughing. The
laugh is the giveaway. It is Ned. Wonderful Ned. Merry
Ned.

"Neddy-Teddy-Bear," she says, smiling. He has hold of
both her hands and is pulling her up. "Neddy-Teddy," she
says. "Neddy-Teddy."

"Oh ho!" he says, looking at her standing there, still
holding her hands. "You've got fat, Malva. Now's my
chance to beat the hell out of you in tennis."

They both laugh, still holding hands. Out of the corner
of her eye she catches sight of her mother. She sits ramrod
straight. Deep wrinkles—almost furrows—hide her expression. She is looking at Malvina, one hand raised to her
breast, mouth slightly open in protest. She has never liked
Ned.

Never you mind Ned, Malvina says to her mother without speaking; never you mind Neddy-Teddy. You only see the fat boy; you only see him joking. You only see the silly boy who gets into trouble and then laughs.

Meanwhile Ned is talking to her in little bursts, each starting with "Remember when. . .?" and "Hey, remember when. . .?" She is answering him, nodding, smiling, nodding. Not for thirteen years has a human being held her hand.

You only see the chubby boy who steals table wine, she says to her mother. You won't forgive him for that. But now—for God's sake, Mother, I'm forty-five. Going on fifty. Can't you forgive him a bottle of wine?

"When was that, Malva? When was that?"

"Oh years and years ago. Hey Neddy. . ."

"No one calls me that any more."

"Why not? Same old Neddy."

"You too, Malva. Same as ever. Oh Jesus'" He is laughing, his red face bunched up with delight. But there are tears in the corner of each eye. She can also smell whiskey on his breath. It reminds her:

"Neddy, remember the day you stole the bottle of wine from Dad's closet and. . .?"

"Which time? Which bottle?" He shakes with mirth even when not uttering a sound.

"The time we went down to the lower meadow. Just the two of us. And we. . ." How is she going to put it with all these stuffy relatives around?

He is looking at her, waiting, not filling in words for her. Smiling and waiting. Doesn't he remember? Suddenly his head bobs, nodding, taking her offstage.

"And rolled down the far hill?"

She nods, grinning. Neither of them have to mention that they were naked. The memory is there, delicious, clear as an August sky. "Come on, come on," he says, still laughing. "We've got a little party going. Just us kids."

Just us kids. She rolls the phrase around in her head like a candy. Just us kids.

He starts leading her out of the room, holding her hand.

She catches a glimpse of her mother, half standing, mouth open as if saying something, but beyond earshot. Friends calm the old woman, settling her back in her seat.

Ned weaves through the crowd in the dining room and then up the stairs. The house is over two hundred years old and the steps are steep. Malvina is panting at the top.

"Good for the wind," Ned says. His face glows with sweat, red like a ripe tomato. "Get much exercise these days?"

She pauses, catching her breath. For a moment she can't remember whether she does or doesn't get much exercise. How long has it been since she's played tennis? He whisks her into the bedroom—the one she used to share with Carrie, her sister. But there's nothing of hers left. They've stripped it of everything personal, made it a guest-room.

"Look who's here!"

They all look up, delighted. Actually delighted to see Malvina there. They come over and one of them kisses her. It is Jay. The youngest. He hasn't aged half as much as she expected. Thin and sporty in his open shirt and blazer. Him and his fancy mustache that she used to associate with the RAF. Not surprising, really, him being a pilot of some sort.

"Oh Carrie!" She hugs her sister. Carrie married young and had a brood of children. Malvina has never seen any of them. Perhaps it is all that childbearing, but Carrie is now heavier than Malvina. It becomes her. And who is the exotic woman in black sitting in the corner? With tinted glasses. Malvina is careful not to stare for fear it's someone she should know. The others crowd about Malvina, but she keeps glancing over at the mystery woman.

"How long has it been?" they keep asking each other, amazed at the force that has blown the family apart. Jay to England after one year of college; Carrie married and settled in British Columbia; Ned in sales, traveling endlessly around the globe. Malvina herself to South America the year she graduated, marrying Byron in a rush as if he were the last flight out of town. The explosion never stopped.

Like a little universe they've been flying farther and farther apart, driven by some mysterious force. And now, here, for some reason, together again. Malvina keeps holding first one hand and then another, clinging.

"First," Ned says, "a drink for Malvina. We're all ahead of you, love. Way ahead. And you deserve one. What'll it be, bourbon or bourbon?" He is pouring already. "And are you still writing?" he asks her. She doesn't know how to explain it—writing as she does in her head but no longer on paper. Perhaps he can read her mind because he goes right on. "Never you mind, Malva; we'll wait for your epic. We're patient."

"Have you seen anything at all of Byron?" Carrie asks.

"Young Byron is downstairs."

"No, I meant Big Byron."

"They've divorced, you know," Jay says in a whisper.

"Oh, sure. I know that, dummy. I was just wondering what happened to him."

"I've been wondering too," Malvina says. Everyone seems relieved. The bourbon tastes strange and hot after so many years of abstinence.

Malvina sips, knowing that she will be punished for it. But somehow that seems less important right now. Right now it is important for her to make them feel at ease. Perhaps they can all melt into their former selves, faces blurring for a moment and re-forming, younger, as in the movies. Malvina is deeply troubled by the passage of time.

"Young Byron is married now," she says. "Can you imagine? My baby married already and with a child. Married a sweet little thing. Thin as a reed. . ." She breaks off, remembering who it was who came over and spoke to her downstairs. How incredibly silly of her to forget. She tries laughing it off, but it doesn't sound quite right.

Malvina tries to be merry, she writes in her head, but it doesn't seem natural. Everyone looks at her queerly.

"A grandchild already," Jay says, his curved mustache poised over his drink. "Boy or girl?"

"Boy. I mean girl. Girl. They named her Trish. . . ."

She stops, bewildered again. Trisha is her other sister's name. Is she the one sitting over there in black? The one with dark glasses? Is it possible that little Trisha has turned exotic like this? Skinny Trisha with no breasts at all. Short hair and bony elbows. Malvina stares and Trisha raises her hand in greeting. Yes, it *is* her.

Just like her not to shake hands or crowd in. Cool Trisha. Is it possible that Malvina forgot her own sister? Is she that badly off? Malvina's head dives for her glass, retreating. Warm bourbon washes through her.

Diving gracefully like a dolphin, Malvina descends into the amber sea just in time to let the rollers break harmlessly over head. Opening her eyes while still under the surface, she sees a torrent of spray bubbles course downward and she knows that it was a killer wave. She feels triumphant, sliding so gracefully under it, escaping harm. It's a natural talent she has.

"And what is your Byron doing now?" Jay says.

"Same as ever. Export-import he calls it. Actually it's getting cars into Venezuela from the States. They're brought in as used cars, you see, and he sells them as new. I mean, they're *barely* used. It's not entirely legal, but it's more or less accepted there. Of course, he has to give a lot of Christmas gifts, if you know what I mean."

She smiles, feeling very competent. She hands her glass to Ned, who takes it with a courtly flourish. "Byron loves it there. He's enormously successful right now. But it hasn't always been easy. He was wiped out three times, you know. Once he had a partner, a Chilean German, who turned him in. And then there was this Argentine live-in girlfriend who did the books and I had to move upstairs. . . ." Her voice trails off. Something is wrong. She can tell from the way they are looking at her. It was all going so well and then something in their expressions tells her she's slid off track.

"You must mean *Big* Byron," Carrie says gently. "Your ex, Big Byron. Back in the good old days."

"Natch," Ned says. "What's the matter, Carrie, weren't you listening?"

Big Byron? She hasn't seen him in thirteen years.

"How're we doing on booze?" Jay asks.

"A bit low," Ned says, turning the bottle upside down. "But I know where there's some more. The old cabinet." He winks at Malvina. "Just where it always was."

"Look," Carrie says, "I don't think. . ."

"If you're hot for cider, you just help yourself. Join the old folks downstairs and talk over the old days." And then to the others, "I'll raid the cabinet. Jay, you get some ice. Carrie, if you're game, get what you can to eat—cold cuts, pretzels, dog food, I don't care. I'd get it all myself, but it wouldn't look right, would it? I mean on this occasion."

Malvina feels a tremor pass through her; there's something dark and ominous about "on this occasion." But when Ned gets to organizing things, there's no stopping him to ask questions. "And Trisha, you stay here to keep Malva company. Tell her funny stories."

They slip out, naughty children, Carrie tiptoeing with comic exaggeration, descending into the babble of the adult party below. Malvina shuts the door and leans against it, holding the confusion at bay. "That's quite a gathering," she says, trying to smile naturally.

"Watch out for Ned," Trisha says.

"Ned?"

"He's a drunk, you know."

"He's just very social."

"He's a drunk. And he'll get you soused if he can. It's his way of hiding his own illness." She inhales deeply and then lets some of the smoke out of her nose. Malvina wishes she wouldn't hide behind the tinted gasses.

"He's just very social." Malvina is hanging on to the old-fashioned latch behind her with one hand, but she isn't sure now whether it is to keep those below from breaking in or to allow for a quick flight. "That's not a kind thing to say about Neddy even if he does have a few too many."

"Don't excuse him," Trisha says, coolly, professionally, like a nurse who has seen it all. "That's the worst thing for people like that. It's no kindness, believe me. He's a drunk. And it takes one to know one." She turns on a smile, quick and wry.

51

"You? Don't be silly. You don't even have a drink in your hand."

"Know what would happen if I took one drink?"

"What?"

"I'd throw up. They have me on these pills. For life."

"Oh, I'm sorry."

"Sorry? Why be sorry? I'm doing all right. We're doing all right when we're doing the best we can." She seems to be quoting someone. "And how about you, Malva?"

"I'm doing all right," Malvina says and manages a little smile that Trisha doesn't return, so she drinks more bourbon and to hell with what Trisha says. When Ned comes back they will have a lovely little party and to hell with Trisha. Trisha always was a loner. None of them have changed. Trisha used to swim alone and walk the beach alone and later went abroad by herself. And then she married some extremely rich Belgian and that was the last Malvina had heard. They sit in silence for a while. Trisha smokes steadily.

"What's this about you writing a book?" Trisha asks at last.

"That was years ago."

"In South America?"

"In South America. And before that, in college. And later. Whenever I can."

"Fiction?"

"Oh heavens no. Just another autobiography. Except that this one is complete. All the pieces. All the pieces in their right places."

"You wouldn't want that. None of us do."

"*I* do. It's so *unfair t*o keep forgetting."

"Forgetting? It's the kindest thing your mind ever did for you, Malvina."

Malvina falls silent, puzzled. She has always thought of her mind as something sullen and uncooperative. Distant. Easily lost. She can't imagine it capable of kindness. What did Trisha just call it? The sound from downstairs massages her like the hiss of waves on a beach.

Malvina listens to the sea and recalls summer vacations, climbing sand dunes, running along open stretches of beaches back in the days before summer tourists began coming there. And the brook that they used to dam. Ned devised the plans and she and Jay and Carrie would carry them out. And Trisha—even then she would wander off, alone, a solitary girl even then. Sometimes they would go home at the end of the day and report her lost, but she always returned. No explanation. Accepted her whipping from Courtney without a whimper. Malvina is struck with how unchanged they all are. Malvina compares past with present, writing about herself and how she writes about how she will write about. . .

"Stop!"

"Stop what?"

"I'm not to think of myself thinking."

"Don't then."

"Talk to me, Trisha." Malvina goes over to the bed and sits down opposite her sister. "Please don't just sit there. Tell me something about the past—anything. Tell me about Jay. Is he still a pilot? Still living in England and traveling all over? He seems less dented, somehow, than the rest of us."

"England, yes. Pilot, no."

"What then?"

"He sells shoes. Lousy cut-rate shoes."

"Oh—but why?"

"Sure you want to know?"

"I guess. Yes, I want to know everything. All the pieces."

"He had a wife and a lovely place in Windermere—the Lake Country. A beautiful spot. But dull. And his wife was lonely with him gone for weeks at a time. So she started importing friends from London. Men friends. And eventually it all blew up—Jay and his wife and three of her friends. There was quite a bash and one of the three got his head knocked in. Dead. Another broke Jay's rib with an oar. The whole thing was in all the papers for days. All the details."

"Jay did that?"

"Well eventually they ruled it self-defense, but by that time no airline would touch him. So no more pilot's job. No more wife."

"I don't want to hear any more."

"I didn't think so."

Malvina stands up and smooths the bed as she has been taught. She goes to the window and stands there, looking at the yard and the mulberry trees. There is supposed to be one for each of the six children, but she can only see five. Has hers died?

"You still married?" she says, suddenly turning back to Trisha. "You live in Belgium and are still married?"

Trisha smiles briefly. "Still married. Same man. No scandals. We have a fine place in Brussels—a town house with a garden. And we summer at Lake Como—or at least I do. He has to work very hard. A government position. And he also manages a family estate. Mining, mostly."

"But. . . ?"

"Well, he has a mistress. It's common there, you know."

"Oh Trisha!" This with compassion. Byron had his women too. Mr. Worldly Wiseman, she used to call him.

"Don't 'Oh Trisha' me. I knew perfectly well that's the way it would be. I wasn't dumb. I don't like to be crowded. I have my summers in Italy and as many trips back to the States as I want."

"Then what happened?"

"Happened? Nothing. I'm still married. I'm always there for the social season, which is all he asks; and my French is perfect—for Belgians. We're a beautiful couple."

"But the drinking. . . ?"

"Oh, that. Well, it was pretty bad for a while. I mean, there was a time there when I almost died."

"The Valley of the Shadow of Death," Malvina murmurs, but Trisha goes right on.

"So I had to learn how to handle it. Zero tolerance. You have to learn your limits. That's all it takes."

"That's all there is?"

"I said, 'That's all it takes.'"

It sounds to her like "That's all there is." Malvina feels inexplicably on the edge of tears. The door flies open and Ned comes in with two bottles. Carrie is right behind him, giggling, with ice in a serving dish and half a ham that she holds in the crook of her arm like a baby; and then Jay with boxes of crackers and bottles of soda and a black bearskin car robe left over from their childhood. They used to sneak out of bed and snuggle under it on the bathroom floor and tell ghost stories.

"A picnic," Jay says. "The teddy bears' picnic."

"Where did you find the old robe?" Malvina says, delighted.

"A little memorabilia from antiquity," Jay says. "A piece of the past."

Then they are all talking at the same time, arranging the car robe in the middle of the room, sitting down on it, setting up the bottles, the ham. Jay pulls a load of home-baked bread from under his blazer and tears it into hunks. And cheese. Malvina spills her drink, but it's all right because everyone laughs and lets it soak into the rug. "Keeps the moths drunk," Ned says, pouring her another. Jay starts reciting:

> The Owl and the Pussy-Cat went to sea
> In a beautiful pea-green boat.
> They took some honey, and plenty of money
> wrapped up in a five-pound note. . . .

He has a resonant voice and a rounded half-British accent. She has forgotten how marvelous he is as a performer. As soon as he finishes she claps, crying out, "'The Jumblies,' Jay. Oh please do 'The Jumblies'!"

"Right-o," he says, more British than ever. He begins again:

> They went to sea in a sieve, they did;
> In a sieve they went to sea.
> In spite of all their friends could say,

> On a winter's morn, on a stormy day.
> In a sieve they went to sea. . . .

On and on through all six verses. And each time he comes to the chorus, they all join in:

> Their heads are green, and their hands are blue;
> And they went to sea in a sieve.

By the end of the last verse they are in a tight circle, arms around each other, rocking back and forth with the gentle swell of the sea.

> And in twenty years they all came back, —
> In twenty years or more;
> And everyone said, "How tall they've grown!
> For they've been to the Lakes, and the Terrible Zone,
> And the hills of the Chankly Bore";
> And they drank their health, and gave them a feast
> Of dumplings made of beautiful yeast. . . .

The sun is hot on her cheeks, the gulls laugh and circle overhead in the absolutely blue sky.

"For God's sake!"

Who said that? Malvina looks up, heart pounding. Dead, dead silence. They are looking toward the door. Malvina turns. It is her brother Courtney standing there, looking down on them.

"What are you doing with Malvina? Are you *crazy?*"

Trisha, glass in hand, lets out a music-hall guffaw, a marvelous throaty, cascading laugh. "You'd better believe it," she says. And then she doubles up tight, spilling her drink, retching on the bearskin rug.

Malvina feels herself bundled up like a child. She clings to the stair railing, trying to stay, but Courtney cracks her wrist, breaking her grip, wrestling her down the stairs, cursing all the way. She's in for a whipping this time. No doubt about it.

At the foot of the stairs she sees all the grownups staring at her. No one says a thing. Just staring.

Malvina dreams that everyone is staring at her, but it is only a dream. Malvina imagines that she has created a great scandal. But she is mistaken, of course. She has imagined this scene merely to dramatize and illustrate her basic sense of. . . Of what? You tell me, Doctor. Of what?

"How could they?" Her mother is working her way through the group, a path opening for her. She uses her cane, but moves with a sureness of former years, majestic. She stands in front of Malvina now.

"Malvina. Listen to me. Do you know what has happened today? Do you remember the service?"

"Never mind, Mother," Courtney says. "I'll take her back."

"Don't tell me 'Never mind,' young man. Malvina, I have to know. Do you understand what happened today? Are you *responsible*?"

Malvina looks at her mother and sees that she is dressed entirely in black. She remembers with sudden clarity the funeral service. She recalls watching a brown moth on the carpet by her feet flutter, rest, and flutter again, trying to fly. She remembers how the minister kept clearing his throat. She remembers standing at the grave-side, studying the fake grass carpet that was designed to cover the bare newly-dug earth but fools no one.

"Well?"

"Yes, I remember. We buried Dad. He's dead. Is that-what you mean?"

Later, in the car, driving back to the home, she looks over and is enormously relieved to see that it is Trisha at the wheel. It is night, and her face looks ghost white in the light of oncoming cars. Her eyes are still hidden behind those tinted glasses.

"Oh," Malvina says, "I'm glad it's you."

"I had the feeling you didn't want Courtney driving you. Do you remember hitting him?" Malvina shakes her head. She would never under any circumstances hit her own brother. Trisha has things mixed up. "You've got quite a punch there," Trisha says. "I thought from that that maybe you didn't want to go back."

"I'm quite ready. I know my limits."

I know my limits, Malvina says, recalling a phrase she heard years before on a summer picnic. How kind, she thinks, of memory to withhold some things and to return others according to one's needs. She feels a rare sense of gratitude toward her own mind.

"You're very kind," she says, speaking to her mind as a friend.

"Sometimes," Trisha says softly.

THE DEATH OF LITTLE GLORIA

Little Gloria stands up slowly, unsteadily. Her knees tingle. She covers her mouth with both hands as if to hush her breathing. There is no way to hush the tolling of her heartbeat.

No, no, no, her mind's voice keeps repeating, but the chant has no power. It will not change matters. For the first time in her life, strength has suddenly been flushed right out of her. Not just from her body. From her mind. Instead of seeing ahead, seeing what has to be done next, it's like the light has gone out.

At sixteen, Little Gloria's body is no longer little. She is actually taller than her mother. Tall and gaunt. Except for her small, hard breasts and smooth skin, she could be the ghost of her mother.

Her mother's sickness took a long time. Little Gloria did everything she could, but the sickness had a life of its own. It was not easy to witness the pain. Little Gloria wished she could take on some of it for her mother, share it, become her in some way.

On one of those long nights when her mother miraculously stopped coughing for a couple of hours, allowing the exhausted woman to sleep quiet as death, and Bro slept too, curled on his cot, Little Gloria played a game all by herself. Quiet as a night spirit, she left the trailer and went out to the yard with a tin cup. She filled it with ashes from the circle of bricks. The bricks were what they used for a stove when they could no longer afford to fill the propane tank. Back inside she turned on the bulb in the kitchen and took down the mirror from the wall. She propped the mirror up on the kitchen table. Working carefully like a movie actress she dusted gray ash in her hair bit by bit until it was the color of her mother's. Then she mixed ash with water and drew worry lines in her face with a toothbrush handle. It took time, marking, erasing, then marking again until she got it just right.

The house was silent that night except for the deep breathing of her mother and the wheezing of Bro who was six and sometimes had to gasp for air what with the desert dust. Occasionally a coyote in the far distance would start to sing, and she—surely a she coyote—would get others to join in a chorus. Little Gloria liked the way they joined together, gaining strength in song. For much of that night she sat in front of the mirror, listening to the family breathing and to the songs of distant coyote families, and stared, unflinching, into the future.

But now, this chilly morning, the future has gone blank. Just flickered out. Now she is feeling something altogether new. Weakness. This is what weak folks must feel day after day. Like the sullen, dark-skinned kids in the school she tried to attend years back, like the chinless man who cleans the toilets at the Unocal Interstate Truck Stop and Diner where her mother also worked—the man too weak to make decisions, too weak for anger, too weak to move away from Unocal where they let him live in a shack. Trapped there in that little island of harsh light and oil smells in the middle of the desert. As Little Gloria stands there with the first cold light of dawn frosting the desert and chilling her butt, the empty hole she feels is so deep it gives her a new bond with those who work at Unocal—folks who seem drained of life. Folks who have drifted there and cannot find the strength to move on. She used to shrug them off, but now she understands how terrible each empty morning must be for them. Shivering, she feels a warmth for them.

"Li'l Gloria," Bro croaks, groggy from sleep. "Li'l Gloria." That's what everyone calls her to separate her from her mother, Gloria. There was a time back before memory when her mother had been called Gloria-Lee to keep from being mixed with *her* mother, but that was long before Little Gloria was born.

"Keep your voice down," Little Gloria says.

"Why?"

"Something's happened."

Bro sits up in bed, naked to the waist. He is thin like Little Gloria. "What? What's happened?"

"Momma's dead."

Bro opens his mouth, but it's like he doesn't know what words to put there. And why should he? He's never been in a rusty trailer in the middle of the desert with a dead woman before.

"Dead?" he finally manages to say.

"You heard correctly."

Bro looks over at the bundle of bedclothes across the room from where his cot is. Their mother, lying on her side with her hand under her cheek, doesn't look any different from when she is sleeping. Except now there is no wheezing. Earlier, in the darkest depth of the night, Little Gloria heard the wheeze stop with a snort. Many times in the past the wheezing and gurgling, water slopping about in her lungs, would miss a beat; but then it would start again. This time it hadn't.

Little Gloria had felt her mother's wrist for a faint surge like the traveling nurse once showed her. There was nothing. She tried feeling for the beat on the neck. Nothing. Then she listened with her ear to her mother's mouth, close as if Mother were about to whisper one last story. Nothing. She even dug her fingernail hard into her mother's wasted arm. Nothing.

"What do we do now?" Bro asks.

"You just do what I tell you to do," Little Gloria says sharply. "And don't ask questions."

"Jeez."

"And don't cuss. Not all day, you hear?" Bro nods. "So first you wash up with the rag there, and then put on your church pants and shirt. I'll find them for you."

"Then?"

"Like I told you, don't ask questions."

It will take him fifteen minutes to get washed up and dressed in the pants and shirt their mother bought for him back when they tried going to the Pentecostal Church in the tin building off Exit 307. It didn't last long, those trips to the Exit 307 Pentecostal Church, Mother driving them in their old pickup. It didn't last long partly because of the heat under the tin roof and the stink of unwashed bodies, but mostly because of the terrible noise.

"Us Stocks," Mother had said, "are tight-lipped. That wailing is no way for folks to act no matter what."

"Us Stocks" is what she often said, referring to the family she was born into. She had two other last names, but she never made use of them. Little Gloria's actual father, the one that got shot because of money, was called Hurley, but her mother never used that name. It didn't stay with Little Gloria either. She was still Gloria Stock like her mother. And her grandmother. It was always "Us Stocks from Oklahoma," as if that were a breed that set them a notch above folks from California. "I didn't ask for life on this here interstate," her mother said more than once, "but us Stocks don't whimper. And we don't wail on Sundays or any other day, you hear?"

Bro washes at the kitchen sink, shivering with the coldness of the early-morning water. By noon the tank outside they fill by hose will be baking and the water hot as soup, but right now even the sun is weak. Think, Gloria says to herself. What comes next? She teeters on the edge of panic.

On hot evenings back before her mother's sickness turned bad, back when her mother would sit silently at the register at Unocal taking money from truckers, her head high as if she were a queen dealing with subjects, Gloria and Bro used to watch TV on the big screen that ran day and night over the beer and wine cooler. Little Gloria learned how other folks live, people in faraway places. She also learned what they do with dead bodies. They pull blankets up over their faces. But Little Gloria isn't about to do that. For two months she's been working hard to get air into her mother's lungs, sitting her up when gunk plugged the tubes, thumping her back when the coughing wouldn't stop. There's no way she is going to cover that mouth and nose now or ever.

"What do we do now?" Bro asks, all dressed up as if ready to go to the Exit 307 Pentecostal Church.

"I told you, no questions," Little Gloria says. "Eat cereal and keep quiet. You're supposed to be tight-lipped, you remember?"

Bro gets his cereal down from the shelf and his bowl and pours water into it. The kitchen is so neat and clean that there is nothing for Little Gloria to do. She scrubbed the peeling linoleum floor last night and scrubbed the walls the night before, waiting for the sun to rise, so there is nothing left to do to the trailer in or out. Little Gloria has never minded that—cooking meals, cleaning up, buying different medicines at Unocal for her mother, taking turns working at the register so the boss wouldn't kick them out of the trailer, teaching Bro his letters and numbers. All that filled the days and nights and then some, with just enough left over to do to make her jump out of bed the next morning, getting to work while the sun was still weak over the desert. But today is different. It's like the sun just hangs there, motionless, wan and feeble like the chinless fellow at Unocal who walks about with his mop like his batteries are all but run down.

It's like the highway just stopped for her. No concrete ribbon, no white line. Just sagebrush. And Bro is asking what comes next.

"Now we have rituals," she says suddenly to Bro as he finishes the last mouthful. She is astonished. It's as if someone else has spoken. A voice has entered her head and has said "Now we have rituals" without her having the slightest idea what it means.

"Oh," Bro says, rinsing out his dish. "Rituals." He doesn't know either, but he has faith that she does. Little Gloria feels a jolt of panic go through her like when she touches the old toaster with wet hands. But then she makes out the route just barely. In the swirling sands, she can just make out what comes next.

"First we pull the curtains," Little Gloria says. "And then we light candles." She says it like they do this every year. Like stringing electric lights over the door at Christmas.

Bro is eager to help. He too must be afraid of doing nothing. He gets stubs of candles they have salvaged from the Unocal Truck Stop Diner after Christmas and she lights all twelve. They'd been saving them for something. This must be the something.

"Help me move her on her back."

Bro hesitates, but Little Gloria yanks him by the shoulder. The woman died on her side, and it doesn't seem right to Little Gloria that the dead should be lying like someone asleep. Her mother should be on her back like on TV, with her arms crossed. They tug, but to their astonishment the body that was once their mother is stiff as a dummy from a store window. They get her rolled on her back, but she was sleeping with her hand against her cheek, so when they get her rolled over she looks as if she is about to call them for dinner.

"That's the way it's supposed to be," Little Gloria says to Bro. "Now get the stool and sit right there beside the bed."

It's a stool they found next the freeway, his favorite for doing his lessons. Well, she thinks, this will be like that, like doing lessons. She pulls a chair over from the dining table so they are lined up, the two of them, right beside the bed. With the curtains over the windows, it is like twilight in the trailer, like the beginning of time, and the candles flicker like stars. Little Gloria wonders if maybe she should eat some food to keep from thinking weird like that, but there are important things she must do first.

"Now listen," she says, as if she is about to drill him on what times what equals what. "And pay attention." He nods. She clears her throat. "This is the story. A long time ago before any of us were born—like in the very beginning, there was this big storm. There was so much dust you couldn't see your fingers in front of your face. Birds fell from the air, choked. Cows turned to clay as they stood. People were drowning in the dust."

"How do you know?"

"I was told it. And now I'm telling you. So shut up. Anyhow, there was this special woman who knew what to do. She packed up her whole family into a truck along with two dogs and two goats and two hens—two of each— and everything they owned. She drove and drove."

"How could she see?"

"She didn't. She couldn't even see the hood of the truck. It was complete black. She just drove and drove, like she was following a voice."

"In the storm?"

"A voice in the storm. That's what she was following. After forty days and nights they came out of the dust. The sun started shining. When she saw that sun shining, she knew she was in California. You know who that was?"

"Momma?"

"Momma's momma's mother." She said it really slow so Bro could understand. "Momma's momma's mother. Your great grandmother. Gloria Stock. Out of the wilderness into the Promise-land. That's what they call this where we live. They had to work hard because that was part of the promise. You understand?" Bro shook his head. "The promise Great-Great-Grandmother Stock made was that if He let them live, they would work and stick together. So that's what they did. That's why it's the Promise-land."

"Where is she?"

"In the beginning she was Great-Great-Grandmother Gloria, and after a while she became Great-Grandmother Gloria, and she became Grandmother. And then *she* became mother. Like that."

"But. . ." Bro hesitates, looking uneasily at the frail figure on the bed there, her white hair all wispy, her hand to her cheek as if calling them. "But, Little Gloria, what. . ."

"The story isn't over," she says, and as she speaks, the very force of the telling creates a text, gives her pages to turn, pulls together a past she has heard only in fragments, gives her a story with pages without end.

"What happens next?"

Turning the page of her own story she sees the next

scene revealed there; she sees what must come next. She sees that they cannot stay there without being turned over to strangers, being separated, losing the story. She sees her mother's driver's license that reads Gloria Stock, she sees a pickup that runs.

"Blow out the candles," she says with a sudden urgency. "Open those curtains. Pack everything into the pickup, everything we own. Hurry before we're caught up in the storm. We're heading out of here."

"Where, Little Gloria?"

"That's another thing—from now on, call me Gloria. Little Gloria is dead. Do you understand? She's dead." Bro shakes his head. "You will. We're getting you into a school somewhere, and you're going to have more school than any of us. You'll get to use words on paper. And when you understand how Little Gloria died, you'll write me a story how it all happened, you'll make it all happen again and again with your words, again and again without end."

Her energy surges back. They pack everything they own, stow it all in plastic bags in back of the pickup. She writes a note giving her mother's name and age, asking that she be buried proper, leaves ten dollars from the stash under the floorboards, and they head out.

Gloria starts humming a song from TV. Bro joins her, knowing the tune but not the words, the two of them sharing the melody. She drives hard and sure, her eyes straight ahead, following a voice.

APPARITIONS

Some time in August Christina Bates arrives in the town of Codman, Maine, near where her daughter and family now live. Still dazed by her trip across the country by bus, she has no idea how many days it has taken. Much of the time was spent in meditation. On two occasions she managed to re-enter her former life as a dairymaid. It's always a pleasure to forget her tall, angular body and Virginia-Woolf face and to recapture at least briefly the plump, easy-going simplicity she had centuries ago.

She had expected the bus to stop at the train station the way it used to, but the driver told her the station was gone. She smiles, thinking of the old station, jealous, perhaps, of all those trains coming and going at will, tired of just sitting there, suddenly working up a head of steam and whipping down the tracks on her own. They've replaced it with a harsh little Arco Station, but at least it has a telephone.

She looks up car rentals in the yellow pages. One company is called Hertz. It sounds vaguely familiar. The other is called Bliss Rentals. What kind of person would, if given a choice, select something with a name like Hertz?

The car looks very much like her own back in California —small and dented. The man apologizes about its having no door handle on the driver's side, but to her this is a friendly touch. Immaculate cars with no evidence of former lives always make her feel uneasy.

The main street of Codman won't stay still for her. What she sees is steady enough, but the time frame has a way of flipping back and forth. One moment it is the early 1940s just before the war and she is a skinny city girl seeing all this for the first time after a long drive, tense with uneasy expectation, pebbles rolling around in her stomach; then time skips and she is a lanky grownup who, much to her astonishment, has turned fifty and is a grandmother. The pebbles are still there.

She doesn't mind the time warps because she is more or less in control. When decisions have to be made, she wills herself back to present. No, not *the* present; it is more a matter of selecting which present she wants.

It is not clear why she had to come. It has been months since her daughter Tony migrated from west to east along with husband Josh and Bojo, their oldest friend, the two children, the goat, and the dog. They'd been having a rough time of it in California, designing and selling jewelry to folks who already had too many trinkets, so they agreed to take over the old Bates place back east and start over. No one else in the family wanted it, so it was theirs for the asking. Tony was never much for letter writing, but there'd been brief notes to say the old Volkswagen bus had made it and they'd moved in. Not exactly warm and grateful as you might expect, but that was her way. And there certainly wasn't a suggestion that Christina visit. A blessing, really. The grandchildren are always fun, but Tony's competence is off-putting. Such bustling efficiency. A disappointment for Christina, her daughter's insensitivity to the spiritual dimension. Faulty genes, perhaps, passed on by her father. But the girl still has years to go. If she doesn't fully blossom in this life, there's always the next.

If Christina ever knew what made it so clear that she must come these thousands of miles, the knowledge has succumbed to diesel fumes and toxic food. She certainly isn't one of those restless women who fill voids in their lives with travel. Her life in northern California has been growing steadily more harmonious over the years. Back when she was married she went through some frantic trials, but eventually she learned that they had been placed there for her instruction. Like the ordeal of being a mother. But blessedly they passed, leaving a new calm. Now she keeps things in balance—going for long walks by herself, meditating, doing Yoga, and working as a freelance illustrator in long, irregular periods of concentration. Her pen-and-ink greeting cards are sold in San Francisco, and from time to time she is asked to illustrate a children's book. When she gets involved in a project, she sometimes forgets to eat for twelve or thirteen hours. Food is such a demeaning addiction. She looks forward to being a star in some distant galaxy so she can simply shine quietly and consume herself, reflecting on previous lives. But until then, she is content with her corner of Mendocino County.

She does not think of herself as impulsive—though divorce lawyers had claimed so decades ago—so this trip continues to puzzle her. She picks at it like a scab. She tries to recall how and when the call to come reached her. All she can remember is waking up feeling very needed and phoning the bus company. Some dream had spoken to her, no doubt. By late that afternoon she was on her way, though the dream had long since wafted away like morning fog.

From the start it seemed important not to telephone. She doesn't want to alarm them or be disruptive. It's best simply to appear, touch them again, give support, and then to leave. It would be like when they lived down the coast from her. Except, of course, that this is farther. She'd forgotten about that.

Now she drives slowly out from Codman to the old Bates farm on Farthington Neck that they have taken over. Someone behind her honks, then passes in a swerving, hostile sort of way. She shrugs. This stretch of country road is hers, energized with layers of her life. She isn't about to let harried folks speed her up and blur it.

There's the elm! Probably the last of its tribe on earth. That's where her father got the flat tire on their way to the farm the very first time. It must have been just before the war—him having the gas to drive up from Massachusetts. She smiles and hears him get all flustered about being late. "Your Uncle Ike will be furious. Goddamned no-good tire." Even as a kid she knew that he was angry with himself for not checking the tire—as if that would make a difference. She knows now that tires blow when your inner self is out of harmony with the world. But what did she know then? She was only an eleven-year-old cousin from Dorchester come for a summer visit.

The car automatically turns right onto the dirt road. It must have taken this route before. And there, almost hidden in the briar and brambles, the old sign, "BATES—KEEP OUT!" She doesn't read the sign, she hears it. Literally. The voice is Uncle Ike's. Hearing him again after all these years is kind of nervous-making.

She slams on the brakes, skidding in the dirt ruts, stalling the car. With her eyes closed, she hears him say those very words again. Not just to her; to all strangers. Like in the story—"Fee-Fi-Fo-Fum." And then he says, speaking to her father now, "For the love of God, Bill, why don't you feed her? That's the scrawniest, palest excuse for a girl I've ever seen. Jesus, I wouldn't even hire her as a crab picker." She lets him play that line over once, twice, tingling with fear and with awe. What is it about pale, skinny girls that makes them take that abuse? And end up almost loving the abuser! She hears his laugh—half Santa and half ugly giant in his castle. She shudders, recalling his tyrannies over the years, his countless injustices against children, women, and pets. In a flurry of rebellion she beats the steering wheel as she once struck at his chest with both fists, shouting "You're mean, mean, mean!"

When she opens her eyes, there is an old Volkswagen bus in front of her, its bumper not five inches from hers. It hasn't driven there—she would have heard it. The big, rusty thing just materialized. Strange, too, that it is so familiar. How many Volkswagen busses are there in the world with antlers from a dead deer bolted to the front?

The driver looks like a walrus—bushy mustache and massive body. He is tapping on the steering wheel the way people do in restaurants when the service is slow. She knows the expression from when she was a waitress at the Golden Onion where customers were real laid back but you could push them to the brink of anger if you tried a little space travel to pass the time.

She starts the motor and shifts into reverse when the walrus shakes his head and gets out of the bus. As soon as she sees his big belly and that rolling gate she knows that this is Bojo and that the bus is the one that brought them all out here. It's strange seeing it here in the land of her childhood, Uncle Ike's realm, where Christina spent her summers and fell in love with her cousin and finally fled to California with him to have a baby before body or soul were ready. She shakes her head in wonder, grinning. How beautiful it is seeing those jigsaw pieces suddenly slip into place.

"Well, hallelujah," Bojo says, peering in at her, his rough face warm as sunlight. "Is that really you?"

"Sort of. I guess. Just thought I'd drop by."

"Christina, honey, that's one long drop, but you sure are welcome. Fantastic. Josh and Tony will be knocked over when they see you."

"Everything O.K.?"

His smile flickers off for an instant and then flashes on again. "You know us—we're doing just fine. Wait till you see the place." He starts to tell her how great the old farm is, forgetting that it was her summer home long before he was born. She nods, not correcting him, still thinking about that flicker of hesitation. She's always liked Bojo—a jovial innkeeper from the fourteenth century—but he's a mighty poor liar. That's one of the appealing things about him— she can see right into his psyche and he doesn't mind. So different from Tony that way. And from Josh too. Two of a kind. But right now it's big, easygoing Bojo who is playing evasive. "And the kids?" she asks, interrupting him. "They're well?"

"Hey there, Mumsie, we're all doing just great. You know us, one big happy family. And healthy. Watch out for those worry lines." She can't help smiling. "Now look, I've got to get into town before the lumberyard closes, but you go on in there and make yourself known. Tonight, we'll have a blast."

She backs out to let him pass and then continues down the ruts toward the farm. She frowns, then turns the frown off in an act of will. He's right, worry brings on disorder.

Minutes later Christina enters that familiar space where

71

the dirt road ends in a grassy yard between the barn on the left and the clapboard house up on the ridge to the right. She gets out, half expecting Uncle Ike to bellow from the barn, "Well hell almighty, look who's grown up tall as Sheba!" Or maybe Aunt Ella will come to the back steps and, smiling, wipe her glasses on her apron—a gentle, wordless way of saying that she can scarcely believe what she sees.

Instead, nothing. No greeting. Then she hears hammering and the wail of bluegrass music from the barn. That would be Josh—as good with carpentry as Bojo is with engines. She heads down there to see him, knowing in advance just how the conversation will go. He'll be pleased to see her, and after talking about her trip he'll tell her how he likes fixing up the old place, how glad he is the family didn't sell it to strangers. Then he'll tell her once again how they are turning the barn into a work studio for their jewelry work. It was Tony, the only one with art training, who'd taught them both, encouraging them to give up selling plastic jewelry and Hong-Kong watches on the street. The words will be friendly, positive, grateful. As will Tony's. But like junk food, all these reassurances will leave her unnourished.

She wonders if maybe it was the children she'd come to see. They change skins so often at this age that photos show kids that no longer exist. Maybe this whole trip was just to get fresh images of them. Is that what happens when you get to be a grandmother?

Thinking of them, she turns and heads for the house. The true front door is on the other side, facing the sea, so everyone uses the back. It has been lifetimes since she has been here and yet some details are so vivid in her mind it's as if she had never left. The massive stone steps, for example, that rise to the back door—those marvelous slabs of granite that absorb the sun's warmth even when the grass is still wet and cold to bare feet. She is not at all surprised to see her girl-self standing here in her bathrobe, just back from the outhouse, toothpick arms clutching herself, shivering and naked under that robe, letting the delicious sun-warmth work its way up through her bare soles. For two hundred years kids must have done the same. Nothing, she thinks, nothing people-built in California has lasted like this—except maybe the missions.

With a nod of gratitude Christina mounts the steps and enters the kitchen. Both children are there—Cliff and Hanny crouched over a copper cauldron on the floor, meticulously shredding bits of lettuce into it.

Hanny looks up. "Hi!" she says. "You want to see Dracula?"

Cliff looks up. "Hey, I didn't know you were coming."

"Who's Dracula?" Christina says.

"Come see."

And from the bathroom—"Who's that?" Tony's voice.

Christina can faintly remember when there was still no plumbing. They used the outhouse—Uncle Ike, Aunt Ella, and all eight cousins. Younger kids used the two-holer together, but at ten or so they got shy and waited to use it alone. Even when the toilet was added, Christina preferred the privacy of the outhouse.

"We found him under the back steps," Cliff says.

Christina drops to her knees and looks into the cauldron. Under an array of garbage is a little green snake. She—her face is unmistakably female—looks right at Christina contemplatively, her tongue darting with nervous energy. Trapped, yet taking it all in stride. Waiting patiently for her moment of escape. What confidence!

"Was she between the rocks out back?" Christina asks. "They love it there."

"Who *is* that?"

"It's me," Christina says, but she can't shout because she has her head in the cauldron and doesn't want to terrorize the snake. "Does she like lettuce?"

"We can't tell. We've only just put it in. It sure doesn't like bananas."

From the bathroom, "Who?"

"Guess who's here," Cliff says. And to Christina, "We tried flies, but it doesn't even look at them."

"Yuck. Who would?"

The toilet flushes and Tony flings the door open. She seems irritated. That figures. Competent people don't enjoy mysteries. Christina is still on her hands and knees and, looking up, is startled at how unchanged Tony is here in this new realm. She still seems girlish with her sandy hair and freckles, yet everything she does is sure. Without meaning to she sometimes make Christina feel awkward and disoriented.

Tony's expression turns to amazement. "Mum? For godsake, where did you spring from?"

"Just materialized," Christina says.

Tony shakes her head. "One of these days, I'm going to believe you."

Laughing, she goes to the back door and calls Josh up from the barn. Then she holds Christina at arm's length the way you might look at a bolt of fabric, cocking her head to one side, her face showing amused astonishment. Then, drawing Christina to her, she kisses her cheek—as close as she ever gets to her mother.

"Seriously," she says, still smiling, "how did you get here? And why? I mean, it's great, but. . ."

Josh arrives, frosted with sawdust, and does a comic double take.

"You sure are a spooky lady, you know that?" He hugs her and expresses delight. The dog, Jose, has come up with him and barks, jumping up on her with desperate enthusiasm. Christina scootches down so he can lick her face, knowing how much dogs like that.

They show Christina around the house, pointing out what they have done and what they plan to do. Actually, most of it is still in the future since they have so little money. Christina tries to show interest, but it would be fine with her if they didn't do anything to the house.

Bojo returns with lumber, shingles, and beer. No, he didn't think to get more food, but they'll work something out. He opens a brew for everyone, but it is Josh who remembers that Christina doesn't drink liquor and pours her a glass of fruit juice. They all ply her with questions—how long did it take her on the bus? What did she eat? How long she can stay? Cliff wants to know what route the bus took and how many hours driving time. They have all forgotten that she is not good at numbers. Details escape from her head like swallows. The children want her to see their pet frog upstairs and their tree house and will she play Hearts with them the way she used to? Christina promises to do all that—but later. She feels buffeted with all this attention. With relief she hears Bojo announce that he will dig mussels for dinner and that Cliff has volunteered to go with him.

There is a lull and she is about to say that it would be nice if she could spend a little time meditating. She hesitates, recalling that flicker of exasperation on Tony's face at the mention of meditation, that slight lifting of the eyes heavenward. In that moment of hesitation Josh offers to show Christina the partially completed studio in the barn. She is swept along, leaving Tony and Hanny bustling about in the kitchen.

Christina hardly recognizes the converted barn. She wants to explore the unchanged corners—the stall where Uncle Ike kept the last remaining cow, the hay loft where Jay convinced her that her body was really beautiful and from where, years later, they were driven from Eden by a wrathful God. Dear Lord, the hay is still up there, waiting sweetly for the next generation.

She wonders if this is something that would amuse Josh, but the past doesn't concern him. He is swept up with the present and the future. He gives her a lecture tour of the studio where they will design and assemble their jewelry, sounding as if he were instructing a seventh-grade class. He means well, but his enthusiasm for their new studio has made him forget that she came to see people, not things.

Such commitment! It was Tony who gave him that, making him dissatisfied with huckstering junk to tourists, teaching him how to do beautiful work. Like many converts, he can't let go. Bojo manages to keep things in perspective, a hungry orphan boy happy to play uncle in this family; but Josh is wound up in a clutter of plans and expectations.

She can remember living like that—what she calls her frenzy years. Decades, actually, when she was leading five or six lives, partnering on and off with Jay even after their divorce, befriending young musicians, experimenting with space travel, being super-mother from time to time to make up for the days she forgot, discovering spiritual teachers to heal the wounds and open new ones. Lucky for her that Tony was one of those self-contained children—getting her own breakfast, keeping her grades up, never asking for a thing.

Josh is talking fast, whirling with energy. A match for Tony. The two of them have a knack of dealing with high voltage without getting burned. He makes her weary with his forays into the future.

When they return, the kitchen is a bustle of activity. Tony is being a super-hostess, baking pies and bread and chopping greens. Christina never makes much of food, leaving it unseasoned and mostly raw, knowing that it drains spiritual energy, but this doesn't seem to be the time to point that out. They are making so much of her being here. Too much, really. All she wants is to slide into their space for a few days and see where she's needed. Perhaps she could watch the children some night the way she did from time to time back home. But here they are treating her like an honored guest. Are they getting gentrified? Or is it the distance she traveled? Maybe they're sorry for her. No, not likely. If they were really thinking of her, they would have given her time to meditate. But it has never occurred to them. It's their way to keep busy. And now they are sweeping her into it, setting her to chopping onions and carrots, peeling potatoes.

Bojo returns with a whoop and shows everyone the mess of mussels he and Cliff gathered, the triumphant hunter returned. Bojo and Josh clean the mussels, passing each one to Hanny, the Official Inspector, who puts the clean ones in the pot and returns the others with indignant reprimands. The men discuss shingling the roof—how long it will take, whether they should hire a helper—shouting to be heard over the Pointer Sisters, June, Ruth and Anita, who have joined the group complete with backup, all in a manic mood. Cliff takes a turn washing mussels so Josh can season some wine for the sauce. When the men put the mussels on to steam, Tony complains that they began them too soon, that her pie won't be ready. Nor the bread. She is told not to worry, that everything will come out all right, that great minds are at work.

Bojo opens another beer, but everyone else is drinking wine. The children have theirs watered. Bojo passes a joint around to the adults. Only Christina abstains, a caution she has maintained for ten years now. Back in her cluttered days there were high altitude trips she took without maps and sometimes it was only through the intercession of the Great Anima that she found her way back at all. She's a cautious traveler these days. The last thing she needs is rocket fuel.

The kitchen is growing hot and steamy. The walls inch inward. Bojo and Hanny are making a big leafy salad. Josh is reducing his mussel sauce and seasoning it from an array of herbs and spices. He has lists of ingredients on three-by-five cards and works like an alchemist.

"Hey, Pal, loosen up," Bojo says. "Let the spices flow."

Bojo loads pepper and garlic powder into the broth, but Josh, laughing, grabs Bojo's wrists and they wrestle. Seasoning flies like spring pollen and both men double over with sneezing. The dog barks, leaps, hoping for scraps, and gets pepper in his face. He puts his head down and rubs both eyes and everyone laughs. Bojo opens the lobster pot to smell the mussels and his head is enveloped in steam. When he reappears, his beard glistens with moisture. Christina pauses in her slicing, startled, seeing Neptune standing there. Where's his trident? The room is getting very crowded.

The kids have provided Dracula with raw mussels,

sliced into snake-sized bites, and pepperoni. "Here," Bojo says, giving them a shot glass filled with beer. "A tankard for your friend there. On the house."

Tony grabs two potholders, opens the oven door, and takes her pie out of the oven. "Hey," Josh says. "Let me. You aren't supposed to be bending over and all."

"Good God," she says, smiling but with a hard edge to her voice. "I'm only four weeks into it." There's a sudden dead spot in the conversation. Tony, the pie in her hand, droplets of sweat on her upper lip, turns to Christina. "I guess we didn't tell you. I mean, it's no secret."

"What's no secret?" Cliff asks. "About the baby?"

"Christina didn't know," Tony says. And then with a yelp she sets the hot pie down on the wood stove. "They don't make potholders like they used to."

As she turns, she stumbles over the cauldron that holds the snake. "Will you take your goddamn friend out of here," she says.

Bojo extinguishes the roach on his tongue, a trick that always makes Christina wince, and puts it back in a little tin box. He spins Tony around in a quick polka, but he can't get her to smile. Turning serious for a moment, he cups Tony's face in both hands. "Wait till you taste my mussels," he says. "They're so fresh they still think they're out at sea." She grins, kisses him lightly, and then tells the kids to get moving and set the table.

Even when they are all settled around the dining-room table Tony can't stay still. She keeps jumping up to attend to things—getting the corn, serving the bread, turning the oven off, turning the Pointer Sisters into Cindi Lauper. The conversation swirls like summer squalls, laughter rising like gull cries. Josh and Bojo discuss which kinds of jewelry to enter in the craft shows and which to interest retailers, what kind of heat to install in the barn. Bojo describes where he and Cliff found the mussels. They wonder about making some spare cash with clam digging. Christina wants to ask Tony about the pregnancy, but hesitates, wondering if maybe she just imagined it. No one seems concerned. The children flip shells at each other, Bojo joins them, and Tony stops the game with a quick, harsh word. "Hey kids," Bojo says, "did you know I had two stomachs?" They are amazed. "Yup, one for the mussels and another for that pie out there." Josh pours more wine and describes to Tony his dealings with the dour electrician who is struggling to update the fifty-year-old wiring in the barn. Josh is a good mimic and makes everyone laugh, and the kids discover that the dog loves mussels.

Christina manages to float up to the left corner of the room and to look down on the scene like a friendly little bat, seeing them all interact in their complicated way and seeing her own physical self down there picking at a few mussels and savoring them while beside her Bojo shoves them into his mouth as if stoking a furnace. She is quite content perched up there, hanging from the molding, but they persist in calling her down. "Why on earth didn't you fly?" Josh asks.

Startled, she looks at him. But he's talking about airplanes. "From California? Money," she says. "There's never very much of it."

"Oh Jesus," Tony says, almost to herself, "you too?"

"Things sure are tight around here," Josh says. "Real tight until we start selling."

Christina wonders if she has come all this way just because of their money problems. If so, it is a sad mistake. The only money left in the Bates family remains with her cousins, not her. Like Thoreau, she's content to adjust her needs rather than increase the supply.

"I don't mind taking the bus," she says, fending off pity.

"We drove," Cliff says. He is referring to their trek east the previous spring. "And Hanny got sick."

"I did not."

"And they made us get out of a motel in the middle of the night."

"Because of the goat," Hanny says.

Bojo laughs. "They heard Nannan bleating. You should have seen the guy's expression when he came in and saw all of us and the livestock in there."

"It's not funny," Hanny says. "He tried to kick her."

The men keep on laughing. Tony sees that Hanny is next to tears and quietly reassures her. Turning back to the others, she laughs again and recalls the man trying to pull down the clothesline with all their wash on it and slipping in goat turds. Christina tries to join in but can't quite hear it all because Cindi Lauper is singing so loud, and behind all this talk and music she hears the babble of eight cousins and her Aunt Ella and Uncle Ike right here at the same table, and she keeps seeing her favorite cousin Jay with whom she has shared such fascinating anatomical explorations that she cannot look at him straight on for fear that Uncle Ike will in a single glance understand everything and strike them dead. She never did get used to such noise, such contact, so many voices from different generations all bouncing off the ceiling and ricocheting from the walls, and now Bojo has raised his wine glass and proposes a toast to the cook, but Tony breaks in sharply. "I'm not a goddamn cook!"

Christina feels a chill rush of bad vibes and stands, steadying herself on the chair. "I'm O.K.," she says. "Really. Just a quick trip to the outhouse."

"Use the bathroom," Josh says. But what she really needs is night air. Quiet night air.

As she leaves, she flicks on the light over the back door. But she hardly needs it. The route to the outhouse is so familiar she could take it with her eyes shut.

Once there, safe in that familiar little building, she realizes that she has fled the dinner not at her body's call but for her soul. She sits on the seat without raising the cover and chants softly—"Omm, omm, omm. . . ."

When mind and spirit are finally rejoined, she leans back and listens to the sounds the house makes. The voices meld, rising, falling, some taking solos, then a chorus. That sweet, beautiful house that has seen more birthing and dying than any human could in a lifetime. She breathes deeply—the musky odor coming back to her like an ugly yet familiar old friend. Then she stands, straightens her denim skirt, and steps out into the night.

She starts toward the house, but stops short. There, lit clearly under the globe of light, standing on the top stone step, arms crossed, is herself. Christina. The spindly kid. Waiting there. Not moving. Alone.

How could anyone be so alone, so solitary with all that hum of activity, that clutter of family just behind her? What's wrong with that girl anyhow?

Christina moves forward, approaching herself, disturbed without knowing why. As she mounts the stone steps she sees that the girl is Tony and that she is profoundly unhappy.

"I had to get out." Her voice is hard. "They're too damn much."

"Who? Josh?"

"Both of them. And the kids. And all those goddamn animals. A zoo."

"Oh Tony, then you are pregnant. It's not them, driving you up the wall, it's all your glands."

Tony's anger collapses and, incredibly, tears come to this tearless child.

"It's everything." She puts her arms around Christina, suddenly hanging on. "It creeps up on you. I used to be a jeweler. A designer. With them. The three of us. Real partners. Remember? Well, look at me now. A farm wife. An old-fashioned country farm wife."

"But you're strong. You're so much stronger than I was. Nothing touches you." It is meant as assurance, but it comes out all crusted with resentment.

"Is that what it seems like? Did I fool you all these years?"

"Oh my baby," Christina mutters.

"Please?" Tony says.

"Please what?"

"Please stick around a while, will you? Please?"

Christina nods, rocks her, holding her tightly, astonished at how soft she is. Now, at last, she knows who sent her that call for help and why she had to come.

Part II

Time in Exile

SEE YOU AROUND

It is Thursday, the 23rd, and Chester Kemp is having a lapse of memory. Thursday, the 23rd, and he is on Flight 652. Flight 652, Swissair for. . .

He has the window seat. Below him, gray fields, small towns. Anonymous towns. Patches of snow. He is high over. . .

Germany. Of course, Germany. He is on the Stockholm flight. Chester Kemp settles back in his seat. A sigh of relief. An annoying task ahead, but good to have it all snap into focus again. Arrive Stockholm 5:33 P.M. and locate his brother by 6:30. Take him out to a decent dinner. Have a little talk. Set him straight. To bed early and up early the next morning. Take the 6:10 flight down to Milan in time for a day of conferences. A tight schedule but possible. All reservations confirmed if only the weather holds. A heavy round of appointments in Milan. All possible if they'd just be where they say they'll be. Not likely in Milan. Maybe he'd take the evening off if the right party was there. Nothing sure, with her in and out of the city so much, but maybe. Friday evening and Saturday morning with her, perhaps. Then off again for Zurich. Two full days with the family.

Chester smiles, thinking of two full days at home, thinking of his wife, Olga, whom he loves, a calm and sure woman, the fixed point about which his life turns and turns. But first his brother. His brother with no phone. No fixed address and no phone. A serious talk with him. Heart to heart. Odd, that lapse of memory, losing track of the schedule. But only for an instant. He looks out the window and down and nods. Fields are gone. A great gray smudge of a city. Hamburg. Solid, ugly old Hamburg. Right on schedule.

"Right on schedule," he says in passable German to a

stewardess hurrying by. She nods, says something over her shoulder, but too fast for him to catch. He leans forward, hoping she'll repeat it, but she's gone.

* * *

Chester's brother is not in Stockholm. At that very moment Chester's brother is on the Irish Sea heading east. He is wearing an Irish sweater that makes him look British. Actually he is American. His name is Rollo. He is in the ferry's public room, having a glass of stout. No one else is drinking stout or anything else. Some are staring out at mountainous waves; some are asleep with Mother Sills; a few are hunched over cardboard cups. Rollo is on his way back to London the cheap way.

"Not much business," he says to the bartender.

"Bad times," the man says. Not clear whether he means the economic cycle or the weather. Perhaps both.

"Rollo!" A roar of a greeting from across the room. The sick and the drugged look up. A great bear of an Irishman lumbers across the floor, left foot, right foot, not quite used to being on hind legs, but pleased at the attention he is getting. "Me bloody long-lost brother and how be you?"

The Recognition Scene: a great embrace, slapping of backs, expostulations of love. Tears come to the eyes of old men and nuns. Rollo has not seen his friend Ian O'Hurley for almost a week.

"Father's dying," Ian bellows, still clinging, rocking from hind paw to hind paw.

"And mother?" Rollo asks.

"In a family way."

"Ah the shame of it all."

"The ole man locked up these two years now."

"And little Nell?"

"Off with a bloody Hungarian, a traveling circus."

"Ah, the whole worl's in a state o' chassis!"

At the bar now, ordering up. Ian slaps the countertop in

86

a bellow of laughter that, muddled with the moaning of the wind and the hiss of spray, sounds to the audience like a grown man's cry of despair.

* * *

"Are you sure?"

"He does not exist."

"If not Rollo *Kemp*, try Rollo *Stone*."

"Which is he?"

"Sometimes under the name of Rollo Stone."

Chester reddens. A stupid pun, a childish goddamned thing for his brother to do.

The girl pauses. She is not what Chester thinks of as Swedish. She is prim, mousy hair knotted tight in coiled braids, mouth tight. No smile. Probably not Swedish at all. "Stone," she says, looking through the register. This is the KFUK—their Y. Stark, unadorned, prim as this girl, it is relatively cheap. It is where Rollo often stays. In the taxi crossing the city, Chester planned to make some jocular comment about the name of the place—the initials in English and all. But this monastic lobby and convent face intimidate him. "Stone," she says. "It does not exist."

"He *exists*. You mean, he's not *registered*. 'Not *registered*' is how you say it in English." She nods, understanding perfectly. "He does not exist."

* * *

Rollo Kemp wakes on the train. It is night. It is cold. The euphoria of the Guinness stout and his friend has long since left him. His dreams have been rising and falling on a not-so-merry-go-round. He has not slept more than an hour, which leaves an incredibly dull and long trip ahead to London. At times like these he wishes he were rich and organized like his brother Chester.

The compartment is littered with scruffy luggage tied with string. Rollo carries his camera equipment in picnic baskets and a wicker laundry hamper to outwit thieves. The stuff is all over the seat opposite him. Also Ian O'Hurley. They have the compartment to themselves.

Ian's body is sprawled like a corpse against one corner, legs out in two directions, arm draped over his duffle. He looks asleep, but his eyes are a crack open. He is surveying Rollo.

"C.I.A." he mutters.

"Where?"

"You. I've got your number. Going to turn you in as soon as we're back in civilization."

"Wha?"

"I saw your bloody passport coming through. All this time I thought you were American."

Rollo grins. Reaching into his pocket he hauls out his not-quite-authentic British passport issued to a "Rollo Stone." He tosses it to Ian. Then, burrowing into the wicker hamper, lifting a false bottom, he locates still another passport, this one allegedly issued by the U.S. to a "Chester Kemp." He hands this to Ian.

Ian whistles, shakes his head. "Schizoid," he says. "And are you really the Rollo Kemp I thought you were?"

"The very one—except on paper. On paper, he no longer exists."

"You stole this from your loyal, upright brother?"

"Do I look like a common thief? No, there's this fellow in Amsterdam who does these. Learned during the war. Old-world craftsmanship. Pride in his work." He takes the "Chester Kemp" passport back, examines it like an art connoisseur, then hides it again. "I shan't use that unless I have to. If the law catches up with me after all these years, I figure they'd treat Chester with greater respect."

* * *

At the terminal once again, the real Chester Kemp hurries toward the reservations desk. He passes a window marked CHANGE, stops, and turns back. Then he pauses again, standing there as passengers stream by him on either side. He is trying to calculate how long it will be before he will be needing Swedish currency again. When he is on his regular business circuit, he knows precisely which countries he will be in on which days. Like an astronomer, he can calculate his orbits months in advance. With this knowledge, he can keep packets of different currencies in his suitcase. It saves him both time and commissions. But this week the schedule is becoming confused and uncertain.

He decides against turning in his Swedish currency and heads once again for the reservations desk. Abruptly he stops, turns back to the CHANGE booth. By this time, two other men are standing there. It's senseless to wait. As he heads again for the reservations desk he looks about him furtively to see if anyone has observed him in this state of absurd indecision.

* * *

Ian and Rollo shout at each other, competing with the roar of the underground. It is the last leg of their trip home. They are on the Edgware Line, barreling their way from Charing Cross to Chalk Farm in North London. It is midmorning, and they have all their belongings piled on the bench beside them and in front of them. They have the car to themselves.

"Ai, ai, ai!" Ian is shouting, clutching his forehead as if struck by a bullet.

Rollo is laughing—the sound of a madman.

After all their talk on the ferry and then on the seven-hour train trip from Liverpool and now on the underground, only now have they discovered that they stayed at the same hotel in Dublin for three days and never saw each other. Each on his own urgent mission, they came and went on different schedules, never eating there and never seeing each other. It is incredible. It is criminal. It is a brutal twist of fate.

"Oh I could have used a friend," Ian wails. "I was in dire need, I was."

"No more than I."

Still shouting, speaking a kind of shorthand of phrases, each lays a tragedy on the other. Rollo Kemp has been seeing Irish publishers, presenting a photo-essay of American exiles, former deserters, and resisters left over from the Vietnam war still living in Stockholm, in Paris, in Germany, in Algeria, the faces and lives of men and their women all but forgotten from a forgotten and discredited war. He calls it, *Now Let Us Praise Infamous Men.* No one seems to appreciate the irony.

He spent his time in Dublin spreading out his prints and his text for successive junior editors. After three knockdowns in three days, an editor-in-chief. A good firm. He allowed himself hope. A superb presentation.

At the end, the pause. Then the old man shrugged.

"Will it sell in America at Christmas time?" he asked rhetorically. Then, answering himself, "It will not sell in America at Christmas time."

Ian was no luckier. For years he has been trying to found what he calls a Laing Commune. It is not entirely clear to Rollo, but apparently psychologists and so-called psychotics are to share a home, living together in equality, supporting each other in a kind of brotherhood.

In Dublin, Ian has been trying to rent an abandoned monastery that was advertised in a London paper. But as with every other attempt at this kind of thing, he has failed to rouse the trust and support of landlords, neighbors, local psychiatrists, zoning boards, public health officials, constables, city councils. Anyone.

"Ah Rollo, a man doesn't know how many enemies he has until he tries to embrace them."

They fall silent until the Chalk Farm station. Wordlessly they help each other unload their belongings off the car and onto the creaking elevator that brings them to the surface. Still in silence they begin the trek, their moods gray like the streets and buildings, like the overcast above.

At the corner they look down the street and see their destination, the Roundhouse. That enormous, soot-stained fortress is the base, the home about which their lives turn and turn. Rollo is suddenly conscious of how exhausted he is.

* * *

At that precise moment an SAS jet passes overhead, hidden above the layer of smog, routinely completing a series of turns, waiting for permission to land at Heathrow. There are twenty-eight passengers, one of whom is an American executive of Procter and Gamble, formerly a purchasing agent for the U.S. Army, a man who is happily married in Zurich, entertains a minor indulgence in Milan, supervises the distribution of his company's products in some thirteen countries, and at present is engaged in a family matter that is taking altogether too much time and is making a mess of his schedule.

He has given up on the Stockholm address and is now tracking down a London address: "The Roundhouse" in an unfamiliar section of London. Slums, no doubt. No phone. Just "The Roundhouse" and a street name. Worth a try.

Is he making too much of this? Letting it get out of proportion? No, this is the same dogged determination with which he tracks down delinquent retailers, trucking firms, distributors. Overdue accounts and lost orders are his specialty. He's well known for his dogged determination. Still, it's making a shambles of his schedule.

* * *

"Sleep now? In the middle of the afternoon? Are you daft, boy?"

"I hardly slept at all on the train, Ian. And neither did you."

"Ah, but we've had the exquisite pleasure of total failure, you and I. 'Twas a well-fought battle, but the Blessed Mother was looking the other way."

He is speaking with his manufactured brogue. He was

born in Sydney of Irish parents and educated in Toronto, so he has his choice of accents. He's not always aware of which he is using.

"I'm not up to it, Ian. And knock off the brogue, will you? I've had enough of that for a while."

"Down on the Green are you? Well then, I've just the thing." He pulls a bottle of Scotch from under his jacket. It is a quarter gone already. "Have a few on me, mate, and you'll turn this bloody town to orange."

"Take it easy with that." Rollo wonders if he should take it away forcefully. He's seen Ian in these moods before. But exhaustion comes between him and the gesture. Ian will have to fend for himself. He drags his baskets across the stone floor toward the office he uses as his apartment and Ian hoists his duffle to his shoulder with astonishing energy and heads toward his. It is 3:15 in the afternoon. With luck Rollo can get a good, long nap before it's time to have supper. He wishes he had Ian's energy.

* * *

Chester Kemp has been in a cab for what seems like hours. He checks his watch. It is 3:15. They have been working their way through industrial wastelands. He thought he knew London, but it is clear to him now that he does not. He has an uneasy feeling that the cabby has been driving in circles to run the bill up, but he has no way of being sure.

"That's the Roundhouse up there," the driver says at last.

My God, it *is* a roundhouse. Literally. Soot-stained granite, circular, enormous, it is clearly one of those buildings once used to turn locomotives about, send them out on different tracks.

The cabby stops, accepts his fare, turns, and drives off down a different street. Chester stands there, suitcase in hand, frowning, recording it all: a railroad yard, warehouses, workingmen's pubs, a Jesus-Saves mission. Everything grimy, even the sky.

He sees now that in addition to offices and apartments, the Roundhouse must also have a theater. The outside is plastered with posters for rock groups, musicals, wrestling matches between men, women, and creatures in drag. Some of the posters are in tatters.

He mounts the steps resolutely. He is not prudish and not naive. He is aware that such worlds exist, but he has arranged his life so as to avoid them. His schedule crosses and recrosses thirteen countries, turning, turning and returning once again, and in each city he is able to find a Right Bank.

It is not the area that fills him with a dark and heavy astonishment; it is the fact that his brother has chosen to live in this alien place. His own brother.

Inside, an enormous circular room essentially unchanged from the days when it was filled with steaming locomotives. Perpetual twilight. Stone floor. Grooves where tracks once radiated from the iron turntable in the center. Ceiling high as a cathedral, still soot-stained, a circular opening in the center for smoke. Dank chill. The place cries out for demolition.

Against one segment of the wall, a raised platform forming a stage. Many rows of folding chairs. In another segment, a dingy bar. Little cafeteria tables placed in the middle of the room. One is occupied by three bearded Pakistanis, two in turbans.

Ah, a directory. Little white letters pressed into black plastic ridges as in cafeterias: "Dr. Asham Landoo, futurist, Rm. 23." "Paper Caboose, Rm. 7." "Dr. Ian O'Hurley, Therapist, Rm. 18." Nothing with the name "Kemp." Flashes of relief and annoyance in quick succession.

"Tranz-Continental Documentary, Rm. 19." Possible? Rollo is forever dabbling with documentaries. Worth a try. "Tranz" indeed.

* * *

Rollo lurches out of sleep at the distinctive sound of his door opening. The hinges are rusty and screech. Alarmed, he realizes that he has merely dropped his things and thrown himself on the bed, forgetting to lock and bolt the door. Worse, the man at the door is formally attired: necktie, topcoat, and hat. Scotland Yard for sure.

But no, he has a suitcase. In a dreamlike flash, Rollo sees his father standing there, ready to go somewhere.

"Are you sick?" the man says.

"Chester? Is that you?"

"What's wrong with you?"

"Chester? Jesus, it's really you. There's nothing wrong with me. Why?"

"It's four in the afternoon. How come you're in bed?"

"I'm not *in* bed. I'm *on* the bed. What are you doing here? I mean, hey, hello. How on earth did you find me?"

* * *

Chester has insisted that they share an early supper. Neither of them is hungry, but the ritual seems important. Since there are no other restaurants in the area, they are sitting at a little round cafe table in the center of the Roundhouse's central room. Chester has offered to pay.

He sits there staring at a short, vegetarian menu. It is entirely unappetizing. He keeps his suitcase by his left foot where he can feel it. They read and reread their menus in silence. Chester feels as if he is visiting a friend in the hospital without knowing what's wrong with him.

Abruptly, he plunges into the heart of the matter:

"Father's had a stroke."

"Serious?"

"Serious but manageable."

He explains that their mother is still coping; there's money enough for a part-time nurse. It's a warning, nonetheless. "I thought maybe you'd like to go back. See him."

There's a silence. Then Rollo says, "I'm kind of ambivalent about him. Him and the country too."

"That's a long time to hold grudges."

"No grudges. They've kind of faded out of my life. Just a slightly sour aftertaste."

A shuffling waiter, a giant out of *The Arabian Nights*, has materialized silently. Rollo orders a nut roast. Chester settles on lentil soup and bread.

* * *

Rollo regrets how difficult this is becoming. Perhaps it is because he is still short of sleep. In the silence he plays mental film clips of a hearty, outgoing American father who is forever throwing baseballs, driving the family some- where, taking boys to assorted games. He wants to say to his father, "You weren't so bad, really. You weren't nearly so bad as I thought at the time." But of course face-to-face he would say it all wrong. They would not understand one another. They would stumble, fall silent, say dumb things neither of them believed. Switching back to the present, Rollo feels a wave of compassion for his brother who has made such an effort to come see him.

"Good to see you again," he says.

"Great to see you," Chester says.

"So how's Olga?"

"Olga's fine." Pause. "Look, how about it?"

"How about what?"

"You know. Dad. It may be your last chance."

"I don't think so."

"I'll pay."

"That's not the problem. The problem is jail."

"After all these years? The war's forgotten."

"I was indicted, remember?"

"Statute of limitations."

"Not in my mind." A pause. Then, "Hey Chester, why don't *you* go?"

"I can't."

"Why not?"

"No time. Tight schedule. In this business, they really keep you moving."

"Just like Dad."

Their father worked for American Standard before his retirement. Moved his family every two years. Kept at it until his retirement. Even then he kept switching from Florida to Arizona. Couldn't make up his mind.

Rollo wonders what it would be like to see the old man again, to hear his voice, to touch his hand. Like? It would be like this.

"Like this," he says.

"What?"

"I didn't say anything."

"You said 'Like this.'"

"Did I? Well, I guess I meant seeing Dad would be like this, you know?"

"Like this?"

"Oh Chester, let's cut all this shit-talk. . ."

"I thought we. . ."

"I don't mean it that way. I mean . . . Oh Jesus, Chester, can't we ever break through. Ever?"

He reaches out and seizes hold of his brother's wrist, staring at his face in the twilight; Chester nods, eyes open wide, his mouth opens to speak, his other hand reaches for Rollo's. . . .

"*Hey you bloody bastards!*" The words slam across the Roundhouse, echoing. "Hey you!"

Chester's eyes narrow with alarm; they both turn; there is Ian barreling toward them, almost falling in a great, lumbering gait. He is blind drunk. The start of another three-day bender. "Running out on me!" he bellows as he slams into the little table, sending it clattering onto the stone floor. They and the other customers jump to their feet.

"Ian, take it easy. It's me, Rollo. This is my. . ."

"I hate it," Ian shouts, grabbing Rollo's shirt front.

"Hate what?"

"It. Here. This. This damn place. You." The other customers approach cautiously. "You too, you black bastards."

"Jesus, Ian!"

The Pakistanis move in, making sounds in the backs of their throats. With suicidal instinct Ian turns on the biggest one. At the moment before impact he suddenly goes soft and Gaelic. "Ah, me long-lost darling brother. Be a pal now and lend me a fiver and watch me blow this stinking city apart."

No one smiles, but the fuse has been snuffed out. No one is going to be killed. The Pakistani stands astonished, silent, on guard. Ian shrugs. "A bloody cold world," he says, and lumbers off toward the north exit. "A cold, cold winter. A bloody ice age."

"He'll be like that for three days," Rollo says. "Bar to bar. Around and around until they pick him up." The others turn back to their tables as if this explained something.

"You *know* him?" Chester asks.

"Like a brother. Really a beautiful guy." He sets the table up. "Most of the time." He tries grinning, but his hands are still trembling. He can't shrug it off. He does not know this other Ian at all. And never will. As they sit there, his mind turns this over and over while his mouth runs on automatic, telling his brother that, yes, it was good to see each other and, yes, it will take a long time to get to Heathrow, and, yes, he'd better leave now; right, the plane won't wait, like time and tide; and, yes, he understands how tight his schedule must be, of course, of course, understand perfectly, perfectly, yes, entirely understandable, of course.

Rollo watches Chester cross the Roundhouse, steps fading, form growing faint in the gloom, picking up speed now, disappearing out the southeast exit, on his way already to Milan.

Rollo sits there alone, struggling with an enormous melancholy that he cannot explain. He is drained of energy, chilled.

"Ah!" In a sudden motion, he looks at his watch. He has just remembered an appointment with a man in Kensingston, a Belgian who knows a German film producer. He almost forgot with all this crazy business. Yes, he has time. Just. If he hurries.

A DEATH IN PARIS

In their fifties and experienced in the usual sort of emergencies that arise when traveling, Peter and Constance Albright found that they were far from knowledgeable when it came to burying an American citizen in a foreign country.

The fact was that Victor was dead. It was hard to believe. It was even harder to figure out what to do about it.

The arrangements fell to the two of them by sheer chance. They just happened to be in Paris when Victor's coronary hit. Sibi had found him, but she was far too young and inexperienced to handle the details. For the first time the Albrights realized that although Victor's circle of friends was wide, he had never mentioned having relatives anywhere.

What they needed was the assistance of a long-term resident, someone who would know something about French statutes and Parisian ordinances, someone who would advise them with cheerful, good-humored affection. What they needed—more than ever before—was Victor.

But they did manage to cope. They finally roused a Parisian doctor in the middle of the night to make the necessary pronouncements, notified the police, and got Victor to a mortuary by dawn. Throughout all this they maintained a cool, dispassionate efficiency. One of the qualities Peter and Constance most admired in each other was the ability to cope. They had gone through financial crises, litigations, and periods of marital alienation without hysteria or loss of dignity. This death, while profoundly upsetting, was a challenge to be dealt with step by step.

When the immediate tasks had been completed they returned to their hotel and waited for the American Embassy to open. Constance took off her suit jacket and lay on her bed without pulling down the spread. Just Peter's height, she was two inches longer than the bed. She lit a cigarette and inhaled deeply. "Too late for a brandy, too early for coffee. An awkward hour. I wish. . ." She paused, inhaled again. "I wish we could just go for a sunrise walk with Victor."

It was the first time they had allowed themselves to say anything personal about Victor. For the length of that long night they had dealt with him only as a problem to be solved.

"It's ironic," Peter said. "The poor guy didn't smoke, never drank too much, never got worked up or tense like the rest of us. It's brutally unfair."

"Did you resent him?"

"Envied him. His life here. The tranquility. Why resent?"

"Because I loved him." She looked at Peter quickly and then stared at the ceiling. "You must have known."

"Everyone loved him." He wasn't sure just how serious a confession this was. Something less, he decided, than actual infidelity. Victor had never seemed to have lovers of either sex. His circle of friends had given him what he needed. Still, Peter didn't feel prepared to press her for details. "Everyone loved him," he said again.

At ten that morning they called the American Embassy. Peter was sure that someone there would handle the paperwork. But the woman they dealt with was chilly, detached. The most she would do was to give them names of bureaus and departments that must certify a death, the cause of death, the taxes due, debts owed, the religion of the deceased, and the request for appropriate burial space. It was up to the two of them to do the legwork. What they had first thought would take a morning turned into a three-day struggle with bureaucracy.

One of the problems was that Victor had lived in Paris for well over thirty years without giving up his American citizenship. This in itself was not unheard of, but his residency papers were not "in order." They discovered that the man they had known for years as Victor Springdale was—on his long-overdue passport at any rate—Victor *Winters*. It was the kind of gently ironic joke he enjoyed. The officials were not amused.

During those three days they wandered from office to office collecting in Kafkaesque ignorance an impressive number of documents each of which required signatures, seals, and various stamps. The sheaves were attached rather ineffectively with common pins. It was not until the end of the third day that they finally reached an individual who was, they were assured, authorized to give final approval. Unlike the others, he spoke reasonable English and insisted on it in spite of the fact that Peter's French was passable and Constance's excellent.

"Who, then, is this Victor *Springdale*?" It was a question that had become a refrain.

"We knew him as Victor Springdale," Constance said in French. She found it particularly irritating when waiters or hotel clerks responded to her French with attempts at English. Peter could see a slight reddening of her neck and a tightening of the jaw muscles, signs he knew as danger signals. "We can testify that the two men are the same."

"Two men?"

"One man," Peter said in English. "One man with two different names."

The official, in his traditional dark suit and white shirt, had a striking resemblance to the late Thomas E. Dewey. But then, that was true of many they had met. The man was neither hostile nor stupid, but he was not about to approve without scrutiny a burial and scarce Parisian cemetery space for a foreign national whose papers were not in order. "You've known Mr.—ah, the deceased for some time now?"

"Over twenty years," Constance said, still speaking French. By now her determination not to speak English had become a subtle signal of hostility that was quite clear to both men.

"Twenty-one to be exact," Peter said in English, trying

to be cooperative. They would be in here all day if Constance really got her back up.

"It is cause for surprise," the official said, softly, as if musing aloud, tapping his pencil on the desk top, "that such close friends—friends over so long a span—would be unsure about the name of the deceased and. . ." he shuffled through the papers, "his religion and. . ." tap-tap ". . .even his source of income?"

Indeed, it was cause for surprise. Even astonishment. They had assumed that Victor was a fairly successful fashion photographer who had been lucky enough to have lived on the Left Bank for decades. Yet there was no record of his ever having paid any taxes under either name. He hadn't even registered as a foreign national. It was true that he rarely talked about his past and almost never about money, but that was part of his nature. Modest, gentle, and generous—those were his qualities. With his round face and easy smile, he invited trust from everyone. He had a quiet talent for bringing others together and making them feel at home without ever asserting himself.

They had met Victor on their first trip to Paris some twenty years earlier. After that, neither of them were quite sure whether it was their friendship with him or their fondness for his little group that brought them back almost every spring. Since Victor enjoyed entertaining at home, they had come to know his large studio apartment as well as any in New York. It was spacious, but the section they used the most was in front by the French windows. During the day one could look out on the Rue de Fleurus, just one block from the Luxembourg Gardens. At night, of course, the shutters were closed and the large, scarred, round table served as the focal point. It was around this table that they shared their aperitif, the long, leisurely meal, and the endless talk. Since the stove, sink, and tiny refrigerator were simply lined up along the side wall, there was really no reason to use the rest of the room.

In the background, however, in the darkened interior, was his studio space—two ancient cameras, the bellows type permanently mounted on heavy mahogany tripods, dusty lamps with enormous bulbs, reflecting screens. On the walls one could barely make out fashion shots, some framed and some not, many inscribed. Unlike many Americans, Victor never bored his friends with talk about his professional activities. He was much more concerned with the arts, politics, and the special interests of his guests.

Peter had always envied Victor's gentle, uncharged life. It was a sharp contrast with the pace Peter and Constance had to maintain in New York. Their apartment was in the East Seventies, but Peter spent much of his time—including most Saturdays—at his architectural office on West Tenth Street. He and his two partners took on more work than many larger firms. Constance was equally involved with her job as magazine editor, heading a small publication for women executives. It seemed to Peter that the two of them spent an inordinate number of days in the workplace and too many of their evenings entertaining clients. The only time they could really let go of obligations and be themselves was with their friends in Paris. It was surprising, really, how often that phrase came up—"our friends in Paris."

When the man who looked like Dewey finally approved their collection of documents with his signature, Peter and Constance were too tired to celebrate. They had a quiet dinner and went directly back to their hotel room. "I could hardly believe it," Constance said. "After three days, that fussy *petit fonctionnaire* finally gives us a date and a place. Just like that." She took off her shoes and massaged her feet. "Is there anything we've forgotten?"

"What about announcements? I suppose it's possible that we'll be the only ones at the burial."

"Only us? God, Peter, that's hardly a decent funeral—even for an agnostic. If that's what he was."

"And Sibi, of course."

"Of course. And that mother of hers. Gladys? Gladys Kruger. I'll call them in the morning. I'm really not up to it now. But I keep feeling that Victor should have a big group. One last party."

"How easy it would be in New York—an announcement in the *Times* and maybe just a few phone calls. But here. . . ."

The problem was that while Victor Springdale was one of the most sociable people they knew, his friends were scattered and transitory. A few were models, but he could hardly be described as "in" the fashion set. There were some Americans, like Peter and Constance, but there were just as many English and Continental friends. Some were in the professions, others in business, a few in the arts—he was catholic in his friendships. But because they were from all over, they came and went like migratory birds. They were not likely to read obituary columns.

Peter stripped to his undershorts and put on a bathrobe. Then he wiped out the two hotel glasses and mixed identical drinks—a double shot of Scotch and a splash of water in each. But he left them on the bureau, caught up in his own thoughts. "We've got to get some of the group there," he said almost to himself. "It wouldn't be right not to. . . ." He went to the window and looked out at the darkened city, but that was a mistake. Seeing the deserted street made him think of Victor dying alone. For the first time he felt a chilling melancholy sweep over him. It was an unnerving sensation, almost like fear. There had been times—always at night, alone, battling insomnia—when he had felt this kind of isolation and futility. He turned back to Constance and said with forced energy, "Get a pencil. It's time to make a list of our Paris friends."

Constance, still dressed but with her shoes off, sat in the only chair, a sheet of paper spread on a Paris phone book in her lap. They both had a predilection for making lists. Peter handed her a drink, sipped his own, and sat opposite her on the edge of the bed. In this manner they began to reconstruct the most recent evening at Victor's—the last social gathering before his coronary. Names were not enough; they had to figure out ways of locating these transient friends. As Peter's drink began to smooth out the tensions of the day, fragments of the evening returned to him as if on videotape.

There had been eight—no, seven guests plus Victor sitting around that table, an echo of countless other evenings in that studio. The faces sometimes changed, but there was always a mood of relaxed intimacy. On this night there was only one couple Peter and Constance remembered clearly from other years. The rest were vaguely familiar. Yet by the end of the aperitif they were all knit together as members of Victor's circle—Victor's little family.

"We do depend on you," the overweight Italian said to Victor. Enrico was what everyone called him, but what was the last name? Torelli? Yes, Torelli. He kept insisting that Italy depended on the United States, smiling, gesturing widely, but playing particularly to the Americans. "We Italians inch our way toward anarchy. You have no idea. Our national preoccupation. Kidnappings no longer make headlines. They are like car thefts. And now they are holding art objects for ransom."

"Kidnapping a painting?" Sibi Kruger said. "A *painting?*"

Sibi, a young, aspiring model from Dubuque, was easily astonished. She and her mother had arrived with Enrico, though it was not clear yet which, if either, was intimate with him.

"Paintings, sculptures. Anything of value. The only solution is to sell everything of value to America! Everything. You hold them for us. The Pietà? I can get it for you cheap. Certainly. Or the Forum—perhaps you could set it up on the prairie next to your London Bridge. For the sake of safety, everything must be shipped to America!" And then with an apparent inborn courtesy he gestured to Carleton Fitzwilliam—"And Great Britain, of course."

"On credit, I trust." Carleton was a wine importer from London. He and his "special friend," Chantal, were regulars, though she lived in Brussels. "No room for the Forum, I'm afraid. But all the little stuff. Statuary, Etruscan pottery—anything that hasn't already been smuggled out."

"Smuggled out? You hear what happened to us at

Pompeii?" Gladys Kruger said, laughing, jangling her collection of bracelets. Lean and bony, she advertised herself with oversized jewelry. "Sibi and I picked up a piece of pottery no bigger than a dime just for a keepsake and you know, they held us all night in that crummy jail and even then I had to wire home for money to pay the fine and get out of there. You can't get away with a thing in Pompeii."

"Ah, what a shame you didn't know me then," Enrico said, beaming. "One call and I would have had you out of there. Just one call and the district capitano would have given you his profound apology. In writing. It is true."

"But I *told* Ma it was against the law," Sibi said. She had the unmistakable look of a model—tall with blond hair stylishly trimmed short; but her voice was adolescent and still Iowa. "There were zillions of signs saying it was against the law."

"Don't you worry," Enrico said, "I have some gemmy little pieces from Pompeii I could let you have at, as they say, a *prix d'ami*."

"Enrico is a veritable storehouse," Victor said gently. "Depend on him. By the way, next time you're in Rome, he could serve as your guide too." Enrico nodded. "He would be happy to show you about and keep you out of trouble. He has more influence than the pope himself. It's always good to have a friend in a foreign city. And here in Paris, of course, I'm at your disposal. I'm no pope, but I do have a few contacts."

"Dear Victor," Chantal Thibault said. Her languid charm made women like Mrs. Kruger seem angular and crass. "How long has it been, Victor, five, perhaps seven years?" And to the others, "If it were not for Victor, Carleton and I would scarcely be able to see each other."

It was not at all clear to Peter why that might be true, but it was unmistakably more than a kindly exaggeration. She was not the type to say anything she didn't mean.

Victor merely smiled and shrugged. He didn't like having the conversation turned to him. Instead, he began asking Gladys Kruger and her daughter which fashion houses they had applied to so far and suggesting others that they should now consider. He also advised her about which were the better restaurants in the area, but Mrs. Kruger was far more interested in her daughter's career than she was in French cuisine. She explained to them all why it was that someone with Sibi's statuesque build would be far more appreciated in Paris than New York. This struck Peter as naive, even absurd. But Victor was, as always, quietly supportive.

"You just might be right," he said. "And you clearly have the perseverance—both of you. That's really what it takes—good looks and a lot of perseverance. And friends."

Peter found it astonishing, this soothing optimism. He himself would have warned both mother and daughter that they were walking into a world where outsiders weren't wanted, where not knowing the language perfectly was risky, and where the pay scales were far lower than in New York. Trying to break into the Parisian fashion world would be a bare-fisted fight. Shouldn't someone warn them? But Victor had the ability to make life seem like a musical comedy, and who was Peter to break the illusion?

It was clear that Mrs. Kruger and daughter had much to learn from Victor, but it was not at all as clear why someone like Chantal Thibault would feel so grateful. In addition to her native French, she spoke perfect English with an Oxbridge accent and occasionally shared some wry comment in Italian with Enrico. As for her lover, Carleton Fitzwilliam, his dealings with vintners made him an expert Francophile. Yet for all their apparent sophistication, the two of them treated Victor as their benefactor.

"I have a treat for you two," Victor said, turning to Peter and Constance. "As I remember it, you were about the first Americans in the Pompidou. . . ."

"Thanks to you," Peter said.

"Well, here's another delight for you. The refurbished Giverny. They've done it just right. A real gem. It's a little complicated finding it, but I know a driver, a very good driver, who will take you there for less than train fare. He is not, shall we say, fully licensed, but he will take you there as, well, a paying friend."

It was typical of Victor's arrangements. Somehow he always knew about guides without licenses, restaurants that had just opened or had just moved up from two stars to three, art exhibits that had scarcely been advertised. Such information was particularly surprising in view of the fact that even after thirty-five years in Paris Victor's French was still terrible.

He must have been able to read and understand French fairly well in order to be so informed, but as a speaker, his accent was atrocious. In anyone else, Peter and Constance would have found this arrogant. But Victor being Victor, they excused it as a quirky stubbornness. Besides, it was this very eccentricity that had resulted in their meeting Victor two decades earlier.

They had been on Boulevard Montparnasse, looking for an agreeable restaurant, when they had seen a slightly plump American in the grip of an irate cabdriver. The cabby was speaking French so fast that even Peter could not make it out. Constance, however, managed to pick up the drift and interrupted sharply. Somehow she managed to calm everyone—that is, placated the cabdriver and dispersed the crowd. The victim was not even ruffled.

Peter, feeling compassion for anyone trying to deal with a cabby without knowing French, ended up paying the fare. After introductions they asked this Victor Springdale if he could recommend a good restaurant in the area. Surprisingly, he could. It was an establishment that had just acquired a masterful chef who had quit his previous job with a four-star restaurant on the Right Bank when he discovered that the owner was not French but in fact a Romanian living illegally in France under an assumed name. Victor urged them to try it for lunch—that being the hour. But he himself would not be able to join them. He had just been down to the Algerian district to exchange foreign currency for francs and had apparently lost his wallet to a pickpocket. He hadn't discovered the theft until he tried to pay the cabdriver. Naturally, Peter invited him to be their guest.

Victor, it turned out, was an expert in French cuisine and felt a deep reverence for French wines—a passion shared by Constance. The two of them got along beautifully from the start. When Victor discovered that Peter was an architect, he proved to be highly knowledgeable about what Paris had to offer. He took them on lengthy walking tours of the city, serving as a relaxed and enthusiastic guide. Peter, who until then tended to view foreign travel as more of a challenge than a pleasure, felt at ease for the first time since coming abroad.

Victor, they learned, had remained in Paris after his wartime service as a photographer in the U.S. Army. There seemed to have been a woman involved, but she was no longer on the scene. "Actually it was French cooking that kept me here," Victor said, smiling and polishing his round glasses. "That and a number of good friends."

On their last full day in Paris, Peter and Constance decided to invite him out again. Predictably, they had become increasingly edgy with each other. Enforced intimacy always put them both off. Victor was delighted to hear from them, but on that particular evening he was having some friends in for a winetasting. He regretted that he had no time for shopping, but if Peter and Constance would be willing to buy some groceries, he would expand the wine tasting into a respectable five-course meal and turn a simple little gathering into something a bit more special.

After so many tedious meals by themselves with the inevitable waiting for service, this sounded like a refreshing change. They were able to buy almost everything he had suggested and a good deal more just out of gratitude. What they spent was still less than an evening out in New York would have been.

There were ten, perhaps fifteen people there, a vivid and lively assemblage. Sharing the wine tasting and then the preparation of the meal generated a true *esprit*. Almost from the start Peter lost the sense of being a foreigner, an outsider—a sensation that tended to spoil his vacation travels. Here he was enveloped in the comfortable sense of membership in this lively and varied group. And so, apparently, did Constance. Back in New York they found themselves describing the trip as their best, focusing on that single evening.

The phone rang. It jolted them back to the present. Absurdly, they looked at each other as if one of them should know who on earth would be calling their hotel room at 10:30 at night.

Peter answered and heard a hoarse, faint whisper: "Peter? Peter Albright? Are you awake?" He managed to identify the speaker as Sibi, the model from Iowa, though she seemed to have her hand cupped around the mouthpiece. "Look, could I see you?"

He felt a flash of annoyance. He was tired and in no mood for mysteries. "Anything wrong?"

"Five minutes. Will you still be up?"

"Of course."

He hung up and repeated the conversation to Constance.

"Must be important," she said. "Do you suppose the girl has some information we don't?"

"Not likely. We knew him better."

"Still, she was the one who found him. Maybe she was having an affair with him."

"With Victor?" He shook his head. Victor didn't seem the type. Besides, Peter had always thought of their Paris friends as a harmonious and open group—not one with secrets.

"It's true Sibi had a key, but he gives. . . gave keys to everyone."

Victor's building had originally been managed by a concierge, but in the late 60s she had gone the way of British nannies. As a result, guests could ring individual apartments, but it was up to each apartment owner to trudge down and unlock the front door. Since Victor lived on the third floor, he simply gave out keys—not only for the front door but for his apartment as well. For a number of years

Peter assumed that he was a privileged friend. It was disappointing to discover how generous Victor was with his keys.

So it was not at all surprising that Sibi had been able to let herself in on the evening he had planned to show her the new publicity shots. The original photographs, taken only a month before, were of no use because her mother had insisted that Sibi have her hair cut shorter. But when Sibi went up to his apartment to see the new prints, he was sprawled on the floor, his filet and an assortment of groceries scattered in front of him. He had evidently just entered the apartment after the three-floor climb when his heart gave out.

Peter had never thought much of Sibi, but he had to admit that her response was very much to her credit. She rolled him over and gave him CPR just as she had learned in high school back in Dubuque. When that failed, she called Peter and Constance, asking them to locate a doctor and an ambulance, though she was quite sure Victor was dead. She had not called her mother because, as she explained, "Ma would go bananas."

That was four nights ago. It seemed to Peter more like a month. What they had hoped would be another relaxing vacation had become even more tense and complicated than their working lives.

When Sibi knocked at their hotel door, she was out of breath. "I didn't want to wake the night clerk," she explained. "So I had to climb the stupid stairs. Sometimes they won't let girls visit at night. Frenchmen—they really think dirty."

"What's up?" Peter asked.

"Sorry to make it so late, but I had to wait until Ma went to sleep. She means well, but there's a lot of things she just can't handle, you know?"

"I hope it's nothing serious," Constance said.

"Well, it is. Really. But it's my own stupid fault. I should have thought of this when I found him."

"Victor?"

"Yeah, but it was a weird time, you know? I mean, here is this dead man. . . ."

"It must have been a shock," Constance said.

"You'd think I'd remember what I came for. After I called you I just went back to our hotel. Like a dope, I completely forgot what I'd come for."

"What you came for?"

"The glossies. My photos. He had a bunch of them. With the new hairdo? And instead of looking around for them, I just cleared out of there. I told Ma yesterday she should go up and get them, but she says there's probably some French law against going in a dead man's apartment. She's scared stiff of getting arrested again. I mean, she was sure we were both going to get raped that time in Pompeii. Rape is big with her. Anyhow, she won't go anywhere near the apartment, and she even made me throw the key in the river like in the movies. She says she doesn't want to be caught with it. I swear, she can get real spacey."

With a growing sense of uneasiness, Peter began to see that he was being asked to go up to Victor's apartment with Sibi and locate the prints before the authorities cleared the place out and did whatever they normally do with the property of individuals without heirs.

"At night?" Peter asked. "You want to go over at night?"

"What's wrong?" Then, wide-eyed, "Victor's not still up there, is he?"

"Of course not. It's just that—well, why not during the day?"

"Ma would kill me if she found out I was going. But if we actually got them—well, she'd just sputter. Right now she's out cold. She sleeps like an ox."

"Well, maybe I could go by myself tomorrow."

"Oh, Peter, you'd never find them. He's got a zillion of them. But I know just where mine would be. Besides, I hear they sometimes seal the place up to keep people from going back in. They could do that in the morning and then what would I do? Look, it won't take us more than a minute, really."

Peter sighed. "Oh I suppose."

She sprang out of her chair with a motion more like a cheerleader than a model and gave Peter a quick but firm kiss on the lips. Then she grabbed both his hands and helped him up from where he was sitting on the bed. It was a schoolgirl's gesture, but he caught a quick glimpse of Constance. The tendons beneath her jaw were tight. "We'll *all* go," she said. "Peter's French is not as dazzling as he likes to think, and you never can tell what you might run into."

Their hotel was less than a five-minute walk from Victor's apartment. That was hardly accidental. Being in Paris meant seeing a good deal of Victor, so they had kept returning to the same neighborhood.

The route was so familiar that for a moment it seemed as if the three of them were planning to pick Victor up and go to a café for a cognac and talk. Perhaps others would join them and the conversation would flow easily, guided by Victor's quiet good cheer. Victor never was bothered by the professional anxieties that plagued Peter and most of his friends in New York. Victor never complained about inflation, student riots, terrorist bombings. "Victor's my guru," Peter used to say with a laugh, though the two of them never discussed anything deep.

But that was all gone now. The reality of it washed back on him once again with alarming force. Somehow he'd been betrayed and abandoned.

The climb up the three flights of stairs was dreamlike. The single dim bulb on each landing was on a timer and stayed lit just long enough for them to reach the next switch. Those clicks and their breathing were the only sounds. The air was dank and musty.

They reached Victor's landing just as the light snapped off again. Constance started to grope for the switch, but Peter said there was no need. "I could find this lock blind-folded," he muttered.

It did take some scratching about, however, and when the door finally swung open he pushed it too hard in his nervousness and it swung back against the wall.

"Who the bloody hell is that?" a voice bellowed.

Peter stepped back as if he had been hit, and from behind him Constance shoved forward. Speaking French in her most managerial voice she said. "What are you doing here? We are going to call the police."

The light flashed on and they all squinted. There, on Victor's large sofa bed, was a couple. They were sitting up, both of them, she holding the covers up to her throat.

"How did you get in?" the man said. Just as Peter recognized Carleton Fitzwilliam, Carleton added, "Well, for godsake don't stand in the door. Come in and close it, will you?"

Sibi gasped. "Weird," she said.

"Not half as weird as having you pop in like this," Carleton said.

"If you're going to stay," Chantal said in her most gracious voice, "would you mind turning about for a few minutes? We're not exactly dressed for company."

Peter, Constance, and Sibi turned and faced the door. They could hear the other two padding about, locating clothes. "This strikes me as positively morbid," Constance said. "Surely you've heard about poor Victor?"

"We heard," Carleton said. "Terrible shock."

"Wednesdays are our day to borrow the place," Chantal said. "It's been a tradition of sorts whenever we're in town. Victor would have approved—one last time."

"Goodness," Sibi said. "What on earth for?" And then, flustered, she added, "I mean, why not hotels?"

"Hotels require passports."

"So what?" Peter said, indignant for Victor's sake. "No Parisian hotel is going to give you a hard time about that."

"It is not the hotel that would object," Chantal said. "They merely record the facts. But I would prefer not to have my name on the books. I am married, you see, and my husband is a very harsh man."

"Victor understands," Carleton said. "Understood, that is. And we've always made it up to him. All the wine you've enjoyed here is from my account."

"Victor did that once for us too," Constance said, her voice still resonating disapproval. "He let us sleep here when our hotel reservations were fouled up. He said he'd stay with friends."

"Of course," Carleton said.

"Well, he didn't. An acquaintance of ours saw him sitting in the Gare du Nord at six in the morning. He was unshaved. He'd been there all night."

"Good Lord," Chantal said, "do you suppose all those times. . . ?"

"We're proper now," Carleton said. The three by the door turned around. Carleton and Chantal looked as if they were ready for another one of Victor's informal dinners, but Carleton's face was dark as it never had been when Victor was alive. "Now what is all this about?—all of you barging in here in the middle of the night."

"It's kind of my fault," Sibi said, opening wide architectural drawers one after another, her back to them. "I'm awfully sorry," she muttered. The drawers were stuffed with photographs, many of them curling. "He took a new batch of glossies. With my new hair style. You like it?"

"Your hair?" Carleton asked. "At this hour?"

"Oh, wow, here they are." She started looking them over, one at a time, cocking her head to one side. "Nice. Really nice. I mean, I couldn't even submit new resumés without these."

"I could have recommended other photographers," Chantal said. "Ones that are better known."

Sibi lowered the prints, letting them hang there at her side. Standing there in the dark recesses of that room without makeup she looked gawky and unsure. "The thing is, we don't have the money. We're practically flat-out broke as it is. We wouldn't even have come abroad at all if we hadn't been introduced to Victor by letter—someone we knew from back home who's over here now driving rich

Americans around Paris. He told us how Victor would help. For nothing—sort of."

"You mean," Constance said, "Victor took all those photographs without charging a fee?"

"Well, he's not a professional photographer, you know. Just kind of a hobby. He got all this stuff after the war. . . ." She gestured to the old cameras and lights. "With what the army gives you when you get out. But he never could make a living out of it. I mean, he doesn't even know much French, you know."

"No professional work?" Peter said. "How on earth did he get along?"

Sibi shrugged. "Not very well, really. Ma takes. . . took him out to little restaurants a lot. Sometimes he seemed kind of hungry. That's all we could do for him. And he was so kind to us."

"Hungry?" Constance said. "That's absurd. He was always entertaining."

"Only when someone like you guys bought the groceries. What you left on your plates, he scraped into jars. I used to help him. He said he fed stray cats at the Luxembourg. That's what he said. Of course whoever ate here then owed him a meal."

Carleton shook his head. "He must have had *some* money. What about the rent?"

"Mr. Torelli—you remember him? He sneaks things out of Italy and sells them to Americans he meets here at Victor's. So he paid it. With a little extra now and then."

"Paid his rent?" Carleton said. "In exchange for contacts? What a bloody fraud!"

"Fraud!" Constance said. "You and your wine so you could use his bed. And poor Victor spending nights huddled in a train station."

"My wine, but you two bought the groceries for all those gatherings. You Americans and your foreign aid. What were you buying? I assume you were getting something in return."

"Nothing sordid like a bed." The tendons of her jaw muscles were like cords. "Peter," she said, turning to him, "what's happened? I thought we were among friends. A lovely circle of friends."

"It's death," Chantal said softly. "Death does that."

"Don't be morbid," Carleton said.

"It lifts a veil, death does. Haven't you noticed?"

Peter looked around and saw that they were all suddenly strangers. They would never meet again. How could everything have come unglued so quickly?

"It has nothing to do with death," Carleton said. "The simple fact is that our friend Victor—whom we trusted— was playing what you Americans so charmingly call a confidence game."

"Playing a confidence game?" Chantal said with a touch of a smile. "Dear Victor wasn't the only one."

EXILES

It is Saturday, a French legal day of rest, but Robert Thorley can feel a humming tension in the air. It is Lisette who is to blame. Poor Lisette is making an occasion, a major celebration, out of what should be just a simple meal.

"Please, Lisette, this isn't some fête you know."

"But of course it is."

They speak French as always. He gave up speaking English the year he settled in Paris some seventeen years ago, and he rarely even hears it except in his dreams.

She turns to him, the wax spray in one hand and polishing rag in the other, slight and stylish in her high heels like young housewives in French television ads.

"Your father's first time in our apartment," she says. Then she looks around with an expression of despair, blowing her cheeks out and letting the air escape—"Pah!" as if she wants to push back the walls. "Your father! Here!"

Robert wonders if that is a French characteristic, this awe of parents. His own father is not at all awesome. Tall—even taller than Robert—but quiet and gentle. His father, still a U.S. citizen, has spent the last thirty five years teaching at the American School in Geneva where Robert grew up. Retired, divorced, and recently returned from his ex-wife's funeral in the U.S., Dr. Thorley seems a bit worn down to Robert. Certainly not awesome. Lisette has met him only twice. On both occasions Dr. Thorley was in Paris for academic conferences. With characteristic generosity he treated them to lengthy gourmet dinners. Although those two meals were extravagant gestures for one on a schoolteacher's salary, they were strangely unsatisfying. Their very formality, so far from the lifestyle Robert and Lisette were used to, made all of them stiff. Even Dr. Thorley avoided anything personal, dwelling instead on Swiss academic programs and on European politics in his usual urbane, slightly ironic way.

There must have been a time when he had strong political views. They had originally come to Switzerland
because he had been indicted by the McCarthy committee
in the 50s. But as a foreigner he was never active in Swiss
political affairs. "We're guests here," he used to say.
Besides, he and his politically conservative wife rarely
agreed, and they made a point of not arguing in front of
Robert. Even now, Dr. Thorley skirted what Robert considered the major issues. For the length of those gourmet
meals, the three of them behaved as if they were, with the
best intentions, struggling with a language that was foreign
to them.

This time will be different. His father telephoned from
Geneva, apparently about nothing, and then casually mentioned his upcoming birthday—his seventieth. "Not an
earth-shaking event, but I do find it a bit startling." What
Robert found startling was that his father would mention it
at all. His parents all but ignored birthdays. Just cards.
"We've never been what you'd call a cohesive family," his
father had said when writing Robert about the divorce—on
a Christmas card. When his mother eventually died in
Boston, Robert decided that there was no compelling obligation to go back for the funeral. There had always been a
certain distance between him and his mother. But he wasn't
entirely sure about the decision. Should he have offered to
go along as moral support? So when his father called and
mentioned his birthday in what sounded like a wistful sort
of way, Robert did something uncharacteristic—he acted on
impulse. He invited his father to come down from Geneva,
to celebrate with them, and even to stay in their apartment
a few days. True, they could only offer the couch, but why
not? And to his astonishment his father accepted.

"Why is Sigmund late?" Lisette asks from the kitchenette where she has been most of the day. Sigmund is their
best friend. "He promised to bring a good Burgundy and
flowers. He promised."

"Sigmund will be here. But in his own time."

"His own time!" she says and gives her little cluck of

exasperation, rolling her eyes heavenward. Robert has seen French housewives do that when discussing the cost of living or some local scandal, but no one in all of Paris can do it as delightfully as Lisette.

Robert shakes out the paper and clears his throat as he always does when it seems wise to retreat from a conversation. He is thirty-nine and still technically American, but sometimes he enjoys playing the part of a French bourgeois head-of-family. This little charade was not always a game. When he first moved to Paris in the late 60s, he made an effort to blend quickly into the French professional class. Although he had no working papers, he was fully bilingual and had an engineering degree. With these assets he managed to get a respectable though grossly underpaid job as a draftsman. The position required the traditional uniform: white shirt, dark suit, and subdued tie. While his contemporaries back in the States were dressing like gypsies and behaving like anarchists, Robert sank into the commuting crowd of northern Paris, taking on its coloration like a salamander. No one could have guessed he was a deserter from the U.S. Army.

Lisette gives a yelp and he sees her in the kitchenette sucking her finger. It is not serious, but he too is jumpy and overreacts. "Are you hurt?" he asks, throwing down the paper and going to her. "Please let me help."

She takes her finger out of her mouth and, laughing, shakes her head. "Help?" she says. "Good Lord, no." It's as if he has made a charming but preposterous suggestion. "Out of my kitchen now!"

But he cannot leave her quite yet. He sucks her finger and tastes the salty blood mixed with garlic. It is so delicious that he grabs her around the waist and kisses her. They are interrupted by a male voice shouting, "Mein Gott in Himmel!"

"Sigmund!" Robert says. Sigmund has his own key left over from when he was otherwise homeless. He staggers back into the hallway as if shocked by their display of carnal love.

"Where were you?" Lisette says in French. Sigmund, whose French is still ponderous and guttural, answers in a stream of German, an outcry against their degenerate exhibitionism. Even after all these years, Robert takes delight in seeing a black man spout German like some Nazi general in a wartime film.

Both Robert and Lisette are laughing, but then Lisette sees that Sigmund has neither flowers nor wine and goes at him with shrieks. She releases all the tensions of the day, beating on his chest and trying to rake his face. He puts on an act of sheer terror, protesting his innocence in German. Doors open in the hallway—not for the first time. Neighbors see this handsome black man pick up a struggling French girl, kiss her, and drag her inside. Fortunately, he is a familiar face around there and no one calls the police.

As it turns out, Sigmund has remembered both the flowers and the wine, but has hidden them just outside the apartment door for the sake of drama. He hushes Lisette with a kiss square on the lips that looks passionate but is, they all know, only theatrical.

Robert met Sigmund in Germany when they were both in their twenties—Robert then a draftee in the U.S. infantry and Sigmund the dutiful son of an ambitious but uneducated German woman, serving his time as a university student in training for the law. Each found himself trapped in what he saw as an unjust and immoral establishment.

Robert escaped first. When Sigmund finally quit, he went to Paris and stayed with Robert and Lisette for a month. It was as if the three of them had known each other since childhood.

Strangely, Lisette always lets Sigmund help with the preparations. She pours Robert a glass of beer (always the glass, never from the can "like cowboys"), directing him back to his favorite chair in the living room, and takes Sigmund to the cutting board where he is to slice carrots so fine he could slip them through the eye of a needle. In sixteen years she has never let Robert do a thing in that kitchenette—neither cut a carrot nor dry a dish. He considers himself lucky, yet seeing Sigmund there sometimes gives him a strange twinge of jealousy. Is it greedy to imagine himself sharing the kitchen with Lisette as well as the bed?

At 5:00 that afternoon Robert's father arrives just as he said he would. Somehow he has calculated exactly how long it will take a cab to get from Orly to their apartment even though he has never been there before. He has always been a precise and conscientious man.

Robert feels himself going stiff and formal just as soon as he opens the door. Having spent his adolescent years in boarding schools and his university years in England, he has never acquired an easy relationship with this man. He shakes hands in the Continental manner, wondering if something more is called for. They are, after all, Americans.

Flustered, he hears himself introducing his father to Lisette who knows him perfectly well and then to Sigmund as "Doctor Thorley." The academic title sounds ludicrously formal, so he tries grinning as if he were using it ironically. But to his dismay Sigmund takes it quite seriously. He stands, snaps his heels together, and shakes hands with a kind of bow. "Herr Doktor," he mutters with a deference that is wholly uncharacteristic. Robert has to remind himself once again that Sigmund really is German, that he was shaped by the Teutonic school system before the reforms of the 60s.

"Morse," Robert's father says. "Call me Morse."

Sigmund nods but will not utter the first name. Robert sees that this is going to be a sticky time.

Lisette seats them in three chairs arranged in a tight circle but will not—cannot—sit down herself. Hovering, she asks Morse if he would like an aperitif, and before he can answer she suggests an American whiskey that she has bought just for him, and then plunges nonstop into how good it is of him to come all this way and how embarrassed they are at having so small an apartment and how foolish Robert was to offer a couch when of course the bed is his and *they* will take the couch; they would *like* to take the couch. They insist on it, absolutely.

This is not at all Lisette. It is a former self resurrected from the flat, dull countryside south of Bordeaux in which she was raised. She has nothing but disdain for the life there, describing herself as a prisoner in a village where "one must close the shutters before blowing one's nose." She will not even take Robert to meet her parents, knowing that he will find them "petty, petty, petty." Besides, in their provincial backwardness they will not forgive his being a Protestant and could not in a hundred years understand how she must live with him in sin rather than ask him to convert in order to have a real marriage. She assures Robert that she will never even think of going back and he believes her, but sometimes he is startled at how often she has to reassure him.

Morse asks for a glass of chablis, and that stops Lisette in midsentence. She has no way of knowing that foreigners all over Europe have taken to drinking dinner wine before the meal. But she recovers almost at once and goes to the kitchenette.

Morse, struggling to fill the silence, asks Sigmund what he does. It is an awkward question because Sigmund is housed and lovingly cared for by a French manufacturer, a happily married man with four children whom Sigmund has never met. It is a warm and stable relationship, but not one Sigmund feels free to discuss.

"I'm a poet," Sigmund says, speaking in what Robert likes to call his sauerkraut French. "My goal is to be the first black Goethe."

"Splendid," Morse says. "But is the world ready for its first black Goethe?"

"Sadly, no. I may have to wait a lifetime for the world to catch up."

Morse then shifts to German, a language that Robert has all but forgotten. Apparently Morse has asked where Sigmund comes from because they are soon discussing Bremerhaven. It is only small talk, but Sigmund seems to enjoy speaking his native language again, so Robert feels he should not interrupt. Still, there are many things Robert would like to ask his father—what he does now that he is retired, what it was like to attend the funeral of his former wife, whether Robert did the right thing by not going back to the States for the ceremony. But his father is speaking a different language.

When Lisette returns with a glass of chablis—on a tray, yet—Morse takes it and continues talking German. Perhaps he does not know that Lisette can't understand a word of it. She hovers for a moment and then goes back to the kitchenette. Robert wonders if she really has more to do there or whether she is using the kitchen as a refuge.

He joins her and sees the pint of imported American bourbon she has bought at considerable expense for his father. It is called Wild Turkey. Although Robert has rarely had hard liquor even as a university student, he opens the bottle and pours a splash into a glass. He tries it straight and grimaces. Then he adds water.

"Have you ever noticed," Lisette says, putting a tiny dab of butter on each chilled radish, "how German sounds like hungry pigs." Robert smiles, but Lisette is not making a joke. "It's true. It's the sound of my childhood."

"They spoke German?"

"Pig French. It is all the same. Brutish. You—you wouldn't know about such things."

"You're angry at me? What have *I* done?"

"Is that what they do in Geneva?" she asks. "Drink dinner wine before a meal?"

So it isn't just Robert she's mad at. It's them all. Or perhaps it's the frustration of trying a grande Gironde meal in a petit-bourgeois apartment. He tries to hug her, but she shakes him off. She looks marvelous to him when stormy, though he knows that this is not the time to tell her.

He finishes his drink and shudders. Something will have to be done about this stiff little gathering. He steps into the living room and clears his throat for attention. "Let's go for a walk before it gets dark." He hears Lisette begin to excuse herself, but the last thing he wants is for her to be left here like some French wife, fretting over the meal while the men are out walking. "All of us," he says, looking at her.

Poor Lisette is caught, one hand on the louvered door that leads to the kitchenette and the other reaching out to Robert. He makes the decision for her by slipping his arm around her waist. "It can wait, no?"

And so in minutes they clomp down the three flights, her spike heels clicking like castanets. Out on the street they turn down Rue Des Trois Freres toward the Cimetière Montmartre. It is not, Robert explains to his father, a cemetery noted for its famous residents like Pere-Lachaise, but at least there are no cars there and plenty of birds. In Paris, Sigmund tells them, even the dead are hospitable.

It is between seasons—just a bit raw and overcast. Morse wears a long scarf and cap, emphasizing his angularity. He looks to Robert like a French intellectual. The only one wearing a coat is Sigmund. In all but the hottest days he wears his elegant, dark blue camel's hair overcoat with brass buttons. It was, he has told them, a gift of his "patron."

Robert sets a brisk pace. He will not have them subside into petty small talk. Besides, the whiskey has left him slightly off balance. It is not a bad sensation, but it makes him feel ill-equipped to deal with the demands of being a host. It reminds him of the day he arrived at work without having put on his tie.

The cemetery is almost deserted. They walk farther and faster than Robert had intended. There are no birds. The whole venture begins to seem pointless. Finally they pause at a rise and, looking down across a hillside of monuments, see a small gathering of mourners around an open grave. The family is dressed in the conservative tradition, entirely in black.

"Let's rest," Morse says. Robert is suddenly struck with the fact that his father is seventy. Perhaps he is more frail than he looks. Cut off from family, Robert does not know anyone that age for comparison. Is seventy old? Perhaps this walk has been too vigorous. What if his father has a heart condition? It would be just like him not to mention a word about it to Robert.

"Hey," Robert says to his father, breaking into English, the language of his childhood, "I'm sorry. We could have stopped earlier."

"We have a nice view here," Morse says in French to them all, "of that little pageant down there. In pantomime."

They sit and watch the ceremony, the priest reading, the whole scene in blacks and grays as if in some old, silent film. "I sometimes wonder," Sigmund says, smiling, "where I will bury myself." His tone is subdued but not melancholy. No one corrects him on his faulty use of the reflexive. "Back in The Fatherland? Here in this motherly land? In Africa? No, I think not there. Altogether too hot. Perhaps in America. I have a father in America, you know."

"Ah, Sigmund," Lisette says, "you never mention him. Do you visit him?"

Sigmund says something sardonic to Morse in German and then, shifting languages and tone almost in midsentence, says to Lisette, "The dear man forgot to leave a forwarding address."

Sigmund then reaches into the pocket of his camel's hair coat with a mysterious smile and draws forth the pint bottle of imported bourbon and admires the wild turkey on the label. From the other pocket he extracts four of Robert's sturdy little shot glasses.

He fills each glass with perfect formality as if this is what one always does in cemeteries late in the afternoon. His performance is so perfect that the rest of them are swept into the improvisation. "To life," he says in his guttural French and raises his glass. They raise theirs. Then he downs it straight. The others follow suit. Lisette almost spoils the ritual with an involuntary gasp of pain, but she accepts the second serving without complaint.

Mercifully, Sigmund lets them sip the second round. They watch the group below them. The priest has stepped back and the family members each throw a handful of dirt into the dark opening in the ground. Robert feels severely disoriented. Could the liquor have entered his system that fast?

"There was no need. . ." Morse says in French, breaking the silence without taking his eyes off the little scene below them, and then pausing. "There was no need for you to go back, Robert." They all know what he is talking about. "I explained to your American relatives that there were legal complications. It was entirely understandable."

"I've been wondering."

"I should have reassured you at once. Immediately. But it was a complicated time. A lot of mixed feeling."

"I'll bet," Robert says in English. It popped out in English because he couldn't think of a French equivalent. Or, he wonders, was there an edge to his tone he didn't quite want to share with the other two? "She never thought much of my politics, did she?" he asks, still speaking English. "Never could quite stomach it."

His phrasing sounds harsher than he had expected, but the question has been chafing him. Oddly, it always comes to mind in English.

Morse is quiet for a moment. When he speaks, it is to the others, using French again. "Robert's mother had rather conservative notions. For many years she and I agreed to disagree about many things. She was appalled at what Robert did. She held her tongue—admirably, really. But she came from a military family, and that leaves traces you can't erase. She never could forgive him."

"And you?" Robert feels dizzy—the liquor or perhaps the terrible risk he has just taken.

"Me?" Surprisingly, his father looks amused. "Surely that goes without saying, doesn't it?" And to the others, "I was indicted myself. He's a . . ." He starts to say "un éclat . . ." as in "chip off the old block," but apparently decides that the American idiom will not translate. He settles instead for "un homme de conscience."

"Say it to *me*, damn it."

Morse looks at his son, astonished. "Good Lord," he

says in English, "I've never said this? I assumed you must know. I *depend* on you, Robert. I *depend* on you." And to the others in French, "If it weren't for him, I'd forget why I chose exile in the first place. It would all fade, all those deep convictions. He is my heir."

Robert feels a flood of relief and affection. It spreads through him, warming every cell. He reaches out and grips his father's shoulder as if the two of them had suddenly stumbled into each other in some darkened corridor.

But their exchange has thrown Lisette into some kind of panic. "Forget?" she says to Morse. "You would forget why you left your homeland?" Her French has suddenly lost its Parisian polish and has turned Bordelaise. "Forget all your anger? All those injustices? Does one end up just longing to go back? Is that what happens?"

"Of course," Morse says. "Absolutely. One longs to go back." She looks aghast. "But," he rests his hand on hers for emphasis. "The feeling strikes only once or twice each year."

They laugh, and Lisette, as if suddenly discovering a shared knowledge, kisses him for the very first time.

"Not even that often for me," Sigmund says. "Somehow I have not yet had this longing for what they say was my Fatherland, not even for an instant. Some of us are born as aliens. From our very first cry. All our childhoods we are homesick for a homeland we have never known."

"A phrase," Morse says, "worthy of Goethe."

"Not quite. Give me time," Sigmund says.

"Time!" Lisette cries, her hands flying to her cheeks. "Oh my God! The roast! My lovely meal!"

They struggle to their feet, helping each other up, laughing at their unsteady state. They weave down the little hill past row after row of tombstones. The funeral party is gone. That dark, forbidding pit is now covered over with a green tarpaulin looks almost like real, growing turf. They gain speed and plunge into traffic. Tires squeal and horns blow, but they hold hands, all four of them, and make their own way home, giddy in their fellowship.

THE TEMPTATIONS OF MIKE-0 ANGELO

She is giving the party in his honor. Just a few of his old Boston friends. When she called, he decided that it would be uncivil not to accept. Civility has marked their first year as a divorced couple, and that's worth a good deal to him.

Besides, it's his twenty-fifth birthday. A quarter century. There is no rational reason he can think of why birth anniversaries should be marked, but it pleases him that Annabelle should remember. It's unlikely that anyone else will. His widowed mother had been good at recalling things like that, but she died his freshman year. Not that Annabelle is a mother substitute. Quite the opposite. But still, she did remember.

Michael, turning this over in his mind, is driving his dented little Honda very slowly. The border between Cambridge and Boston is not far—just over the bridge; but he is making a journey out of it. He always drives slowly when trying to make sense of his life. This has probably saved him from disaster—if you don't count rear-end accidents.

What bothers him is that there are equally good reasons why he should have refused—civility notwithstanding. One is that he is not having an easy time of it returning to Harvard after going slack in the real-estate world for four years. He no longer reads with that facile speed that made his undergraduate career such a breeze. And the graduate-school attitude in art history is furrow-browed. Most of his peers are single-minded. They lead lives that strike him as relatively pure and simple. None, as far as he knows, have been distracted by marriage, much less by divorce.

In addition, he suspects that Annabelle may attempt some kind of reconciliation. She won't be heavy about it. She has southern ways that she brought up from Baltimore

and nurtured a bit, and she isn't likely to do more than sprin-
kle the conversation with hints. Still, the prospect makes
him uneasy. A stoplight turns red—a sign from the heavens? But then it turns green again. So much for omens.

"Uh-oh," he says aloud as his car finally turns onto
Byron Street. The short block is made up of converted carriage houses. The one they once rented and decorated, now
hers, is blazing with lights and booming with sound. It does
not sound like an intimate gathering. But then, Annabelle
has always had difficulty with restraint.

At first, Michael is lost in the crowd. There are familiar faces, but they can't quite place him. It's been almost a
year, after all. But then he is greeted by Belva Carlyle, one
of his favorite older friends. She is tall and has
shoulder-length, silver-blond hair as smooth as a ski slope.
When she was younger she was a singer and went on tour
with Bob Hope. Now she is married to a distinguished broker who is an expert on speculative stock and the
Napoleonic wars.

"Michael! I had no idea you'd be here. What marvelous news. Are you back for good?"

"I'm just a guest. It's my birthday."

"What a shame. I though maybe you were in residence
again."

"No, I'm in graduate school."

"You *do* look undernourished. Come by some time and
I'll give you a decent meal."

Older women are forever trying to feed him. Annabelle
used to blame it on what she called his hungry-orphan look.

"Actually, I'm kind of busy. I don't get back to Boston
much."

"Jesus, it's only across the river."

"Seems like a long way."

"You must be dying to see Annabelle."

"I guess I'll work up to it." They smile—she knows
what he means—and he heads for the bar.

The bartender is a hired college student who looks
about thirteen. He is conscientiously measuring out each

drink with a shot glass. Michael reaches behind and mixes himself a heavy gin and tonic—his first hard liquor since the night he told Annabelle he was moving out. He helps the kid out and it is not long before he is taken as the assistant bartender, which is fine with him. It allows him to watch the scene and listen to the dialogue without participating, as snug and detached as if he were watching a film. The place has really never looked better. The other carriage houses in that row had been decorated at considerable expense—one high Victorian, one Art Deco, another what Annabelle liked to call Late Mafia Renaissance. Since Michael and Annabelle were only renting, and his income as a junior real estate agent was minimal, they settled on Industrial Chic—perforated metal racks for bookcases, steel work tables from an appliance assembly shop, seats from junked cars, and a multitude of bare-bulb hanging lamps with green metal shades. Michael had endorsed the plan on grounds of simplicity. But by the time they got through dressing it up with silver and gold radiator paint and Radio Shack strobe lights, the effect struck him as more rococo than he had planned. True, it had individuality, but it was a place he'd rather visit than inhabit. As it turned out, that's exactly what it's become.

"Mike-o!" Annabelle's voice sails high above the hubbub. "Mike-o Angelo!"

She cuts through the crowd with Compton in tow. Round-faced, round-eyed, curly-haired, red-lipped, she has the slightly unreal look of an old-fashioned valentine. Michael recalls a dream in which she managed to float through the locked door of his rooming house in Cambridge, invading his space, smiling sweetly and whispering, "Well, hello there, Mike-o Angelo."

He kisses Annabelle lightly—as if she might be slightly contagious—and then gives Compton a real hug. The two men feel a great reservoir of affection and goodwill for each other—Compton out of gratitude for his new life and love, and Michael because Compton keeps Annabelle happy, warm, and undemanding.

"How are things going?" Michael asks, reverently hoping that all is well.

"Swimmingly," Compton says. "How does the old place look?"

"Anyway," Annabelle says, her favorite way of cutting in, "there's a problem with the kitten."

"Ah yes," Compton says. "The kitten."

Michael is relieved. For while, all of Annabelle's major problems were sent his way for solution—should she stay in the house? Should she accept money from her mother down in Baltimore? Should she take classes and get a real-estate license? Now all those are handled by Compton—incompetent as he sometimes appears. But a kitten—that sounds like a simple, unentangling sort of problem.

"You want a good vet?" Michael asks.

"It's beyond that," Annabelle says. "The thing is that she's fallen in the toilet, got flushed down, and has plugged it up. It's flooding and won't shut off and dear Compton is squeamish about toilets and things."

It's true that Compton has certain limitations that way. Until he moved in with Annabelle, he lived in an apartment-hotel and had never changed a light bulb, much less unstuck a toilet. At the gallery he owns, he hires people to do anything physical.

"How about turning the water off?" Michael says.

"There's a switch?" Compton asks.

Michael heads for the bathroom, followed by Annabelle, Compton, and a trail of camp followers who are drawn by the promise of drama. The unnumbered gins have begun to seep upward into Michael's frontal lobes, softening them, and he gives thanks for small blessings. The kitten is no doubt a goner, but the drama has a drawing power and the bathroom keeps filling with spectators. The wire snake that he is thrusting into the bowl is meeting a spongy resistance. The crowd seems to enjoy the Freudian aspects of the operation. While Michael gets dirtier and sweatier, his audience helps out with witty observations and sound effects.

The older ones have brought their drinks; there is also the smell of grass in the air, which acts like incense. Compton finally offers Michael a toke and that helps to put the probe in perspective.

"The Northstar Scrubber," Elliott Carlyle III is saying, thumping Michael's chest with a thick, stumpy finger. "Most important information you'll receive all evening."

Michael blinks and tries to make sense of it. Somehow his joust with the toilet is over. He has lost an intervening chunk of the evening, but the storm-tossed bathroom flickers into focus, and he is relieved to recall that the kitten was found, live and healthy on top of the refrigerator, and that the obstruction, which he finally pulled out by hand like an obstetrician, was a shoe. Some woman at the party is going about with only one shoe, but apparently she hasn't noticed yet. Michael recalls making some effort to take a shower, but everyone talked him out of it. And now, still damp and slightly rancid, he is listening attentively to Belva's husband, Elliott Carlyle III, who is well known for his prophetic vision of market trends.

"The Northstar Scrubber?"

"The Northstar Scrubber *Inc.* A sleeper. In three weeks—too late. Tomorrow's Thursday. Thursday?"

"Friday, I think. Today's my birthday."

"Friday? Don't wait until Monday. On the phone early tomorrow morning, Michael. Get your broker out of bed. You know what a scrubber is? Eh?"

Michael describes something with bristles at one end and a handle at the other, but he is wrong, all wrong. A scrubber, it turns out, cleans pollutants from smoke and somehow the there's been a dramatic breakthrough regarding high or low sulfur percentages in coal-burning generators. . . The description goes on and on, but all Michael can see is his own favorite nylon backbrush whipping up a lovely mountain of suds.

"Really," he says, nodding. "Really."

"Best move you'll ever make."

"Best move," Michael says, sincerely grateful.

"Really." He wonders what it would be like to have a broker you could call up to arrange your future.

"Have to go," Elliott Carlyle says. "Another little gathering on the agenda. Ballet types. Terribly important to
Belva. She was a singer, you know. Dancers are too flighty
for me, but Belva's drawn to them and God knows they're
safe enough. Come by the house when this thing blows
itself out. I'll show you the prospectus."

"Prospectus?"

"Northstar Scrubber Inc. Don't forget the name."

"I'll remember," Michael says, watching Belva sweep
toward them. Her luxuriant, skiable hair makes her look to
Michael like a film version of Catherine the Great. He
decides she must be decades younger than her husband.

"We've *got* to get going," she says. "Poor Mike-o! I do
hope Elliott hasn't been giving you advice."

"The scrubber. . ." Michael has already forgotten its full
name.

"Oh Jesus! Pay no attention." She laughs and then they
are gone. For a moment Michael feels an unexpected jolt of
abandonment. Like a stitch. But it passes and he joins the
party, sliding easily from group to group. His old friends
greet him warmly. They keep asking whether he's back for
good, treating him like Lazarus.

Hours later they run out of booze. Cries for Annabelle
and Compton—where are their reserves? Those are gone
too. Are the package stores closed? Of course. What to
do? Annabelle jumps on a chair and, putting two fingers to
those cupid lips, produces a whistle that could shatter windows.

"Dear friends," she announces, "we're migrating up the
hill to the home of Elliott Carlyle III—everyone. Bring
your glasses." And she gives the address. Annabelle,
oddly, never drinks much. She can remember addresses and
even phone numbers when all about her successful men and
women are reducing themselves to infancy.

Since there are no farewells, there is no lingering at the
door. The crowd pours out as if leaving a theater, flows

along the middle of Byron Street, glasses in hand, crosses Charles Street, blocking the late-night traffic, heads up the hill, genially inviting drifters and loitering women to join them.

Michael works his way to the head of the procession, intent on telling Annabelle that Elliott and Belva are not home, that they are off at some ballet reception. But by the time he gets there and is greeted by Annabelle and Compton and the others in the central circle of friends and is made to feel like a prophet returning to his people after a sojourn on the mountain, he forgets what his message is.

"Jesus, Michael," Compton says, "where have you been for the past year?"

"Just holed up in Cambridge."

"We need you here." And speaking in his ear so the others can't hear, "*I* need you here. Look, Michael, things are not exactly smooth. We've had some nasty. . .well, you know."

"You're looking great. Things will work out."

"Listen," Compton whispers. "You're seeing us at our best."

"Oh, hey, I just remembered—about Elliott and Belva. . . ."But there is no point in continuing because they are already mounting the stairs to the brownstone and Compton has produced a key left over from some past intimacy. He has a way of collecting keys. So they begin invading the place, taking possession like kindly Goths by simple right of numbers.

The lights in the empty living room have been left on and the tape player murmurs show tunes. The effect is eerie. Michael, whose inclination is to turn off lights when leaving any place, becomes convinced that Elliott must be hiding somewhere in the house. Perhaps he saw them all coming up the hill like an apparition and decided he just couldn't take it any more. Imagine finding your locked door no protection, your personal space violated like this! Michael decides that he should find Elliott and assure him that the invasion is benign, that they are unarmed and mean

no harm. So while the others rifle cabinets, distribute bottles and fresh ice, and pull back the orientals for dancing,
Michael goes upstairs.

The second floor has a sitting room in the rear and a
frilly master bedroom in the front. The lights are on but
there are no people—not even in the bathroom, which
smells sweetly of lilac. On to the third floor, which is dark.
He opens the door to the first room, flicks the switch, and is
startled to find it occupied. Someone is sleeping in a large
bed. She sits up abruptly—a lovely Botticelli woman rising
from rumpled sheets as if from a shell.

"Elliott?"

"Oh, hey, sorry."

He flicks off the switch without introducing himself and
closes the door. Across the hall there is a large room that
for a moment appears to be empty. Then, looking down, he
sees that from wall to wall there are hills, valleys, streams—
an entire landscape occupied by toy soldiers. There are
thousands of them tactically arranged for battle—infantry,
cavalry, cannons—regiment after regiment in Napoleonic
uniforms.

"Please!"

Michael jumps, turns, and sees the Botticelli figure
standing by the bedroom door. She modestly holds a sheet
across her front. She is tall, about Michael's age, with deep-
set almond eyes.

"What?"

"Elliott doesn't want anyone else in the war room," she
says, her voice soft and melodic. "Except, of course, me."

She turns, glides back to the bedroom, oblivious of the
fact that the sheet covers only her front. Michael imagines
what it would be to arrange Napoleon's troops with her, the
two of them on hands and knees, and is struck dumb. Still
trembling, he returns to the living room. He discovers that
the record player has been abandoned and the party has
gone slack. He feels a surge of anxious, unspent energy as
if he were host and this were his show. Crossing quickly to
the player, he takes off "A Little Night Music," puts on a

disco record, and turns up the volume. Then he grabs the hands of a woman drowsing on the couch and begins dancing with her. Her blouse and skirt are a bit too tight for comfort, as if they were borrowed from a younger, slimmer sister. She dances well, though she keeps looking around as if not quite sure where she is. He realizes that she must be one of the loitering ladies they picked up along the way. He does his best to make her feel at home.

Compton—reliable Compton—does his part by swinging Annabelle out of her chair and they join in. Others follow. Michael feels a certain sense of achievement. It's as if he has single-handedly wound up some enormous toy.

He dances in a free style, barely touching his partner, keeping a host's eye on the others. It's his party, after all. He sees Annabelle laugh. A good sign.

But then he frowns. He has just seen Elliott and Belva arrive. Someone welcomes them like strangers, offers them drinks. Belva is amused but Elliott is not. He heads upstairs. She starts to join him. Uh-oh. Michael sweeps his partner into the arms of a lonely-looking art critic and goes to Belva. Better to start her dancing, he decides, than try to explain the Botticelli scene upstairs. He adopts a manic tempo.

When Belva, laughing, pleads exhaustion, he spins her to the couch and, turning, ricochets into Annabelle's orbit, eclipses Compton, and without thinking enters into a routine that they had worked up years ago, the two of them taking center stage.

They exhaust each other, and when the record finally ends they hang there, arms over each other's shoulders like two welterweights ready to call it quits.

"Oh Mike-o," she says, her eyes round and solemn, suddenly looking close to tears, "this is all I want." Her long sigh embraces him, the party, the whole house.

Michael can't respond because his stomach is making what he takes to be a moral protest. In his moment of hesitation the music begins again and Compton, surprisingly surly for an old friend, sweeps Annabelle into dance.

Desperately Michael, hand to his mouth, checks the downstairs lavatory and, seeing the door swing shut, bolts for the stairs and up to the master bedroom. He makes the bathroom there with less than seconds to spare.

An achievement of sorts. He has made it. But his pants have been splattered and need sponging off. He tries a quick job with an embroidered face cloth and scented soap, but he uses too much water and it soaks into the khaki. He can't go down looking like that. Back in the bedroom, he takes his pants off, stumbling a bit, and hangs them with meticulous care over the foot of the four-poster bed. Then, feeling immodest, he puts on a bathrobe from the closet— white silky thing with white fur of some kind around the bottom and the collar. It tickles his ears. Party sounds drift up to him like a distant storm. There is nothing to do but wait.

He feels geological plates beneath him shift. He'll have to sit down if he is going to meet the demands of his rebellious stomach. He retreats to a wingback chair, sinks into its wisteria print, is caressed by its tendrils.

When he wakes, the place is incredibly quiet. "Like a tomb" comes to mind. He can hear a distant clock ticking. Peeking out from under puffy lids, he sees Belva in bed. She holds a magazine and is oddly metamorphosed. Her hair is gone, replaced with a white stubble. Her face is pale as parchment. She is wearing a pair of half-lens glasses he has never seen. She is smoking a cigarette and reading *Vogue*. The familiar, silver-blond coiffure waits for her, disembodied, on the bureau.

She looks up and smiles. "Party's over," she says gently. "Want a nightcap and join me?"

He sees that she has left brandy in a snifter by his chair. It does not look inviting. "I guess I sort of blew it."

"Relax," she says. "It happens to everyone."

"Annabelle's gone?"

"Finally."

"She gets a second wind kind of late." He wonders how long he will go on apologizing for her. "She really enjoys talking."

"The talk I can take, but tonight it was all about you. How marvelous you are, how serious, how you have—I swear it—a soul."

"Good Lord — Poor Compton!"

"Poor Compton is right. If she'd known you were still here, she would have lured you back to that Erector-Set palace of hers. Lord only knows where Compton would have spent the night."

"Out on the street, I suppose."

"To my mind there are some things civilized people just don't do. You don't turn people out on the street in the middle of the night."

"Really."

"I wouldn't dream of turning you out, for example. Not in your condition."

"What's my condition?"

"Lost, lonely, and polluted."

"What about. . ." He finds it difficult to mention Elliott by name, so he points upward.

"Don't worry," she says gently. "He has his toys and I have mine. What the kiddy doctors call 'parallel play.' Come on and get some sleep." She pats the covers beside her.

He slips off the silk robe and slides into bed just as he used to join his mother years ago when thunder, winds, and lightning made a terrible confusion of the night.

He lies close to her, his stomach to her back, his hand cupping her breast.

"You've got everything," she murmurs. "Dear God, I'd give my soul to be your age."

He wants very much to respond to this, but while he is trying to sort out the clutter of his feelings he hears her gentle snore.

Her cigarette, still smoldering in the ashtray, has ignited the other butts. Smoke wafts up from the little pyre. He reaches across her to snuff them out and for the first time realizes how badly the whole mess smells. So does her scalp. And the bedclothes. Pulling back, he realizes he too must have smelled all evening from his toilet work. Why didn't anyone notice?

He rises, dresses quickly, pausing only to take Belva's glasses off her and set them on the bedside table, lens side up. Finding the door locked and the old-fashioned key missing, he slips out the window and makes his way down the rusting steps of the fire escape. The last section swings him abruptly to the sidewalk with a metallic wail that strikes his ears like some defeated dragon.

Then he heads home, driving lickety-split over the bridge to Cambridge with the windows wide open. Under a clear, starlit sky, the magic name comes back to him—the Northstar Scrubber. With a shiver of delight he feels jets of pure water and a hundred little brushes scouring him clean from head to toes.

THE SENATOR'S SON

At one-thirty in the morning Senator Blair Sherman and his young wife Cleo were jolted awake by the wail of the security alarm and the glare of the twenty-three floodlights that suddenly lit the grounds around their Alexandria home. When Blair checked his surveillance monitor he saw someone trying to jimmy the kitchen door with a jackknife. He locked the bedroom door, reassured Cleo, and waited for the police. It didn't take them long. Not until they had the man up against the wall at gunpoint did Blair discover that the intruder was his son.

Once that had been straightened out, the two young officers had to be treated with a certain degree of hospitality. Blair liked to say that for a politician any publicity was good publicity, but there were exceptions. It would not score points if reporters got wind of the fact that the senator's almost invisible son, not seen, photographed, or even mentioned in publicity for a decade, had been arrested trying to break into his own father's home. Not great for the family-values image.

Cleo, a former member of his staff, had been around politicians long enough to know that. Without being asked, she brewed coffee for the two officers, produced sugared doughnuts, and joked with them. She kept her silk robe belted tight, but the young, blond officer couldn't help sneaking looks at her, and the older one tried to impress her with stories about lurid crimes in the D.C. area. By the time they were ready to leave, they would have done anything for her.

"You won't have to write this up, will you?" she asked.

The older one shook his head, grinning. "Those alarms have a way of going off by themselves. Circuit error, we call it."

It was three-fifteen when they finally left. Blair, naked

under his bathrobe, felt like a silver-haired heavyweight at a press conference. He checked his watch, shook his head, and turned to his son as if for the first time.

"Well," he said, "I guess it's time for real introductions. This is Cleo."

"My stepmother," Timothy said. "I kind of figured."

"Hi," she said. "You've got quite a sense of drama." Then, with just a hint of a smile, "Like your father."

It was odd, seeing them together in the same room for the first time, his son and his wife. They were about the same age.

Timothy said, "Your police up here sure are quick on the draw."

Blair nodded. "At least they're on our side. Just for the record—how come you didn't try the doorbell?"

"I didn't want to wake you up."

Blair turned to Cleo. "One thing you'll find out about this boy. He's all heart."

Blair glanced at his watch and realized that he would only get four hours sleep at best. A hell of a way to face the upcoming funeral.

"Drinks?" Cleo asked.

"Too close to breakfast," Blair said. "How about another cup of coffee?"

"Your father's occupational curse," she said to Timothy. "Caffeine addiction."

"Make mine orange juice," Timothy said.

Blair contemplated his son. He had heard that back in Florida his son was living with a good-looking woman, that she worked on yachts the way Timothy did, often shipping out on the same boat. She also, it would seem, was in the habit of serving Timothy orange juice whenever he asked.

All that was hard to imagine. But then, the boy had changed. The same narrow face and shoulders—his mother's genes—but he looked fit. More muscular. A certain self-assurance. And the ponytail was gone, thank God. Apparently being a boat bum hadn't been a total disaster.

Blair had assumed that his son wouldn't come north for

his mother's funeral. After all, he hadn't bothered to show up for Blair's marriage to Cleo the year before. That had made Blair nervous. Some reporter could have dug up the fact that the senator's only son was not in attendance. But luckily Timothy had kept such a low profile since leaving home that no one noticed his absence. Odd, though, that the boy would show up to honor his mother after all these years.

"When I heard that siren," Timothy said, "I figured you'd blow your stack."

"Who said I didn't?"

Timothy looked at Cleo who was at the door, heading for the kitchen. "Did he? He used to curse a blue streak back in the good old days."

"He still can. But not this time."

"What's wrong with him?"

"He's too glad to see you. It's made him all squishy."

Blair laughed. "That's the only adjective the press hasn't thrown at me."

"You'll never get re-elected if you go all squishy," Timothy said.

"What's that to you?" It came out harsher than Blair had intended. He laughed—more from embarrassment than amusement. "I just meant, you probably vote in Florida now, right?"

"I never vote anywhere."

"Very funny."

"No joke."

"What's the matter? Don't believe in democracy?"

"Don't believe in politicians." There was a hush. Blair was used to attacks, but not from within the family.

"They're like regular people," Cleo said. "Just bigger."

Then she excused herself to brew coffee and squeeze orange juice. As soon as she was gone Blair lit a cigarette. He was down to three a day—and these in private.

"I tried to get hold of you," Blair said, inhaling deeply, "but you must have an unlisted phone. You get my telegrams?"

"I don't have a phone. I heard about it on the boob tube. They sure give you a lot of coverage back there."

"We work at it. But it would have been nice if you'd let me know you were coming."

"I didn't know myself until I was on my way."

"No problem. Come along with me. I've got every-thing worked out."

He explained the plan in detail. He was good at details. They would leave at eight in the morning. Blair's driver would get them from Alexandria to Baltimore, and they would wait nearby but discreetly out of sight. Then they would walk to the church just before the service—a brief photo opportunity for the press on the way. Walking responses but no substantive statements. After the service they would leave immediately, avoiding awkwardness with his ex-wife's family. They would be home by early evening. Cleo would wait dinner for their arrival.

"But no chauffeur," Timothy said.

"He's not a chauffeur. He's a driver."

"No chauffeur."

"Why not?"

"I always hated that chauffeur routine. Remember when Richard used to drive me to school? I'd lie flat on the floor of the limo. Hiding. I'll drive."

"Sorry, it's all planned," Blair said. He was used to his own driver—a former New York cabby—and he didn't even know if Timothy had a valid license. "If we do the dri-ving, we'll have to buck the traffic all the way and we'll never find a parking place. Like I keep telling you, the guy isn't a chauffeur, he's a driver. So relax—I've got it all planned."

Timothy shrugged. "O.K., I'll hitchhike."

Blair felt the blood rush to his face.

"For Christsake. . ." he said, his voice louder than he had intended. But Cleo was at the door with a tray with cof-fee, orange juice, and more doughnuts.

"Why not let Timothy be your driver?" she said lightly to Blair. "It's too late for a rousing fight."

The next morning it was raining. Timothy didn't have

a valid license, so Blair ended up driving. The traffic, as Blair had predicted, was heavy. He was strongly tempted to point this out, but he didn't want another argument. They were on their way to a funeral. It ought to be one of those times when father and son do some straight and honest talking. Review the past. Dredge up old grievances. End with a hug.

It had been five years since they had seen each other, and close to ten since Timothy had left home. Even before that they hadn't been close. The boy had his mother's reticence. It looked as if they might make the entire trip without saying a significant thing. It was up to Blair to start, but his mind couldn't let go of the stupid argument about the driver. It reminded him of how willful, even obstinate, Timothy had been as a child. Like the wrangles over posing for the press. Even before Blair first ran for office he was in the public eye as prosecuting attorney, and there were occasions when the press wanted a family shot. From his earliest years Timothy had a nasty trick of crossing his eyes for the camera. When Blair won his first race for Congress, the A.P. photo showed the boy picking his nose. Having his son take off on his own at sixteen without even applying for college was disturbing, but it sure solved some problems. And to his credit, he had never once called home for money.

"It was a tumor?" Timothy asked. He had a clumsy way of lunging into a topic.

"A tumor. Just three months. I would have called earlier if you'd had a phone. Why not get one?"

"I don't need a phone."

"That's crazy. Get one and I'll cover the deposit."

"It wouldn't have mattered. I was in St. Thomas most of the time. And then down the Leewards. I'm all over the place. But I would have come back earlier to see her if I'd known."

"She was in a coma toward the end anyhow. Probably wouldn't have recognized you."

"God." There was a pause. The windshield wipers

pounded. "How about you?" Timothy asked finally. "Must be pretty weird."

"You could say that. Might be easier if we'd really fought. That I could understand. Fights I'm good at. Clears the air. But it wasn't like that. Fay wasn't a fighter. We never had a single argument." He ran his hand through his hair. "Jesus, Tim, back then I was crazy about her."

"That right?" Timothy wiped fog off the windshield. "I wasn't around when you two broke up. What the hell happened?"

"I wish I knew. She just withdrew. I was into my second term. She'd survived the first campaign—not happily, maybe, but that's what marriage is all about, respecting the contract. And she was making progress—shaking hands, making a couple of short speeches. Batting .250, which was O.K. with me. But as soon as the pressure was off she began to withdraw."

"Walked out?"

"No, into herself. Like a turtle. That was a joke, my calling her 'my little turtle.' She didn't find it very funny."

"It's not. But maybe the tumor was getting to her."

Blair shook his head. "I'm talking about eight years ago. She didn't have any tumor then." He switched on the radio. The sound of the wiper blades was getting to him. "I wish to hell it was that simple. There was a lot of stuff going on—like maybe she wanted more children? She said once that I had promised or some such. But politics, in the public eye all the time—that's no kind of life for kids."

"Tell me about it." Still sarcastic.

"She even claimed I'd promised not to go for a second term. That I'd go back into private practice. Live in one place. All that."

"Had you?"

Blair shrugged. "You owe something to your constituents too, you know. I don't think she ever understood that. She never felt—well, committed to the public. Outwardly sociable, but as if she had this hankering for privacy. I never knew what was going on in her head."

Another silence fell between them. Then Timothy said, "Yeah, she always wanted to raise poodle puppies."

"Where'd you get that idea?"

"She told me."

"Puppies! That's crazy!"

Timothy set his jaw. "That's exactly what she thought you'd say."

"I wouldn't have said it."

"You just did."

Blair sighed. "Let me tell you something, Tim. I always did my best for you. You know that? I did my damndest to make you into something solid. I had great plans for you. But whenever I see you, you always want to spar. How come? Because I was away a lot? You know what this life is like. I'm sorry if you felt neglected."

"Actually, I get along fine with neglect," Timothy said.

The service itself was less difficult than the drive. Because there had been a private cremation, there was no box to contend with and not much ritual. His former in-laws were civil enough, no matter what they thought of him. Like Timothy, they buried their grudges too far down to be examined. Blair himself came from farm stock in Arkansas, where people said what they thought straight out and in plain language. He himself had never been on a farm, nor had his father, but it was a tradition he honored. He never had gotten used to his in-laws' Baltimore gentility. He could detect a certain distance, a slight chill in their tone—as if the divorce had somehow been his fault—but there was no way he could defend himself. He much preferred the public rough-and-tumble of political opponents and the press. Politics, he used to tell his wife, is like football. You know damn well who your enemy is.

Timothy was dressed in a pale blue cotton jacket and a white, open shirt with the collar outside—appropriate in Florida but just wrong for this crowd. If the boy had only given him a little warning, he would have had Cleo buy him a decent suit and tie. But of course Timothy could have worn Levi's and none of Fay's clan would have actually said anything. That was the way they were.

Their civility was another reminder of Fay herself. "I'm so sorry," she would say, asking not to be seated at the head table, not to attend a testimonial, not to address a women's organization even after he'd gone to the trouble of writing out every word for her. The worst was when she turned down the opportunity to christen a naval ship after he had pulled strings to get her invited. Fay was soft-spoken and courteous to a fault, but she was stubborn, doing everything possible to stay in the shadows for no good reason. Exposure, he explained to her repeatedly, was at the heart of the game. Pollsters had proven time and time again that the recognition factor often outweighed one's stand on issues. It was as simple as that. But the more he impressed all this on her, explaining it carefully and at length, the more she seemed to yearn for invisibility. Here at the funeral, the anger and frustration he thought he had long since laid to rest rose up and took hold of him once again. Anger, frustration, incomprehension.

After the service, there were a few more mandatory introductions; but as soon as he decently could, Blair gave his son a signal, gesturing toward the car.

"You go ahead," Timothy said when they were outside. "There's some folks around here I want to see." Just like that. What folks? Had the boy kept in touch with his mother's family? Not likely; Blair would have heard. Boat owners looking for deckhands? If Timothy had just mentioned that he'd like to meet some big-boat people, Blair could have arranged it. He knew plenty.

There was no end to what he could have done for the boy over the years if the kid had only asked. When Timothy was young it was a family joke that he could be anything he liked when he grew up as long as it came after law school. But that was only for laughs. Blair would have gotten him to West Point if that was what he really wanted. Anything was O.K., except being the loser the boy had become.

"Be back for supper," Blair said. "By eight for sure. Cleo's got this roast chicken for us." But infuriatingly the boy just kept on heading down Charles Street toward the bus stop, ignoring the drizzle, whistling.

Blair and Cleo ate the roast chicken by themselves. There was no way of guessing what Timothy's plans were. The boy really had no notion of other people's feelings. Like being tone deaf. Was it the divorce that had done that?

After a brandy and a fast scanning of the *Post*, Blair suggested they turn in; it had been a stressful day. But once his head hit the pillow, he was wide awake.

"It's his arrogance," he said, sitting up abruptly.

Cleo sat up too and turned on a light. She was used to these late-night sessions, listening patiently, often at great length, as he unloaded his private rages in the privacy of their bedroom. Once in a while he would in a flash of panic wonder whether her patience would ever wear thin, if she'd quit on him. But she was still young and gave no sign of it.

"Arrogance," he said again. "He really has no concern for others. Or himself, for that matter. He's in a dead-end job. A deckhand! I was through law school at his age. I was in the thick of things. Every other kid with his advantages is out in the mainstream, raising a family and making a name for himself—every one but mine. And why? I can't even get him to talk with me. Jesus, Cleo, he's a total stranger."

"You two aren't so different as you think."

"Are you kidding? We're exact opposites. He's a cipher. Invisible." And then a new thought struck him. "You don't suppose he's on his way back to Florida, do you?"

"Could be. You were hoping he'd stick around?"

"Why sure. I barely saw him. I mean—Jesus, Cleo, he's the only son I've got."

When the doorbell rang at 1:00 a.m., Blair's fresh surge of anger was evenly matched with relief. At least now he could re-activate the alarm system.

"I thought you two would still be up," Timothy said. It was as close as he would ever come to an apology.

"Well, we are now. Cleo's in the kitchen, doing up some espresso."

"Orange juice would be fine."

As they came into the kitchen Cleo smiled at Timothy as if he had showed up just when he was told to. Blair wondered if it was a youth thing—being so easy and loose with schedules.

"How'd it go?" she asked.

"I don't really know how funerals are supposed to go."

"It's supposed to be like closing a door and moving on."

"I did that years ago. Hey, what's with the walls in here?"

He had noticed for the first time that the plaster had been patched in great circles, awaiting a fresh coat of paint.

"Don't get me off on that," Blair said. "I wanted to have the walls painted before we moved in. I had a contract, a written contract, but their labor costs went up or something and they reneged. That really gets to me. A written contract, and they just ignore it."

"Get someone else."

"Not so easy. They're union, of course. And the union's a big supporter."

"Have it done at night. They'd never find out."

"Are you kidding? Reporters would be on the phone the very next morning. They'd make the evening news—local at best, national if they needed a filler."

"God."

"You've forgotten about life in a fishbowl?"

"How do you stand it?"

Blair shrugged. "Some people are just born with tough hides."

"And some," Cleo said, "have to acquire them."

"The thing about Cleo," Blair said, "aside from her fantastic beauty, is that she comes from a political family. She's known what public life is like since birth. It's in her blood. She thrives on high visibility."

"Hey Cleo," Timothy said, "is that really true?"

She had just poured Blair his coffee and looked at Timothy directly. "No," she said. Then, to Blair's relief, she laughed. "I'll never *really* get used to it. Sometimes I think they have this place bugged. If he belches, the *Post* announces that I'm a bad cook. But as the bumper stickers used to say when you and I were kids, 'Love it or leave it.'"

She gave Blair his coffee and slid her hand under his bathrobe to give him a quick, awkward embrace and kiss. "Don't forget that you have an early day."

"So what else is new?"

"Timothy," she said, "it's nice getting to know you at last. I'd begun to wonder if you really existed. You want to hang out here for a couple of days?"

"Sounds tempting, but I don't plan that far ahead."

"Hard to imagine! Right now Blair's booked solid for the next eighteen months."

"That's success for you."

"Don't knock it till you try it," she said with a quick smile. She blew the two men a kiss and headed for the stairs. When she was gone, they were quiet for a while. For some reason Blair recalled a meeting he had attended with a trade mission from China. It had gone fairly well until the woman translator went to the ladies' room. Then the two delegations became dumb and were embarrassed by the silence.

"How about a swim?" Blair said, downing his coffee.

"Sounds good. Got a suit?"

"We don't use suits. Something I learned from Cleo."

"She's good for you."

"How's that?"

He shrugged. "You don't keep trying to shape her up."

As they crossed the living room, Blair put his hand on his shoulder, but Timothy twitched free.

"Damn painters," Blair said. "A contract means nothing to them."

The pool was open but private, surrounded by tall stucco walls. The rain had stopped and the air was muggy and warm. There were floodlights, but Blair rarely used them. The area was dimly bathed in purple light from an oversized bug killer that he left on day and night. He pulled a fresh towel from the stack, tossed it to Timothy, and took another for himself.

"You can't hear the phone or the doorbell from out here. It's about the only place where Cleo and I can be alone."

"Tough life you lead."

They undressed and laid their clothes on two opposing wrought-iron chairs. Then they dove in together, unintentionally synchronized. With matching strokes they started doing laps. Blair began to feel the tensions of the day slip away as they usually did when he was swimming. But when Timothy pulled ahead a bit, Blair quickly caught up and then eased ahead. Timothy increased his speed without changing the stroke, doing surprisingly well for someone who as a kid had never bothered to keep himself in shape. Blair recalled how frustrating it had been, reminding the boy to keep up with morning calisthenics and to show up early for practice. For all the encouragement, Timothy was never outstanding in a single sport. So when had he learned to swim like this?

They reached the end of the pool and doubled back in racing style for no good reason. Blair felt a flash of irritation and began swimming in earnest. At the end of the next lap he was half a length ahead, made perfect contact, and sent himself out like a torpedo. But something had gone wrong. He realized that he was alone. Stopping, he saw that Timothy had got out and was toweling himself down, watching his father with what looked like amusement.

Blair swam a few strokes on his back, catching his breath, and did a final lap by himself. Oddly, it made him feel self-conscious being watched like that. He never minded swimming or jogging for journalists or photographers, but being observed by Timothy was different. There was something very judgmental in the boy.

He swung himself out with a single lunge the way he did when Cleo was there. "You're in pretty good shape," he said.

"You too—for an old man."

"Hey, them's fighting words."

Timothy shrugged. "Strike it from the record."

Blair wrapped the towel around his waist, went to the

bar, and poured a Scotch and soda for each of them. He wasn't going to get even an hour of sleep wound up like this, and the next day was wall-to-wall appointments until after midnight. He didn't want to think about it.

Behind him Timothy said, "Did she hold it against me? For leaving home like that?"

"Your mother?" Blair shrugged, adding ice to the drinks. "I honestly don't know what was going on in her head. Maybe she thought you were well out of it."

"That was the hardest part. Leaving her. I should have told her that in a letter. All those years and I never wrote a real letter. Postcards, but not a real letter. It makes me feel shitty, not having written her."

Blair knew he should reassure the boy, tell him the cards were enough. They hadn't been, of course. And what made it worse was they were all addressed to Fay. It was a stupid little resentment, the kind he normally kept to himself, but it rose to the surface now. "At least *she* got cards."

Timothy laughed. "You would have sent them back— 'address unknown.'"

"Come on, Timothy, you meant the world to me. You're an only goddamned son. You have no idea what I had invested in you."

"Invested? I thought investments were something you owned."

With great effort, Blair let it go. That was always the hardest thing to learn as an amateur boxer—spinning with the punch, letting it glance off, not returning it until just the right moment.

"Speaking of investments," he said, pretending he hadn't understood and returning with the drinks, "she had almost no money, you know."

"What's that got to do with it?"

"I thought you might be wondering."

"I hadn't thought much about it one way or the other."

"You must think about money *some* of the time. You're probably the only kid in American that never asked his old man for a cent."

"I had to fend off money."

"I mean after you left, dummy. You weren't living out of dumpsters, were you?"

"I work. I make good money."

The two of them were sitting at a round metal table with an umbrella over it. Blair put on a pair of dark glasses that had been left on the table, and Timothy put on a swordfisherman's cap, pulling the long visor down. They sat in the purple light as if baking in the sun. Occasionally a bug would snap and fry.

Timothy pointed toward the bug light. "Those things really work?"

Blair shook his head. "Only the dummies get caught. The smart ones circle around without quite touching."

"I hear's there's some that ignore it altogether."

"It's stupid, but it came with the pool. No charge."

"Speaking of money," Timothy said, "you said there was some?"

"Some what?"

"In the will. You said 'not much.'"

"Ah, that. So the profit motive is not dead after all. You had me worried for a while. Yeah, most of it went to her sister. She really needs it. But there's $6,000 for you. I'll have them send it to your bank."

"I'll take cash."

Blair laughed. "I guess you haven't heard, but this city gets the cold sweats at the very mention of delivering packets of green stuff. Seriously, what's the bank?"

"Seriously, there's no bank."

"You that broke? Need a little help?"

"I've got more than you'd believe."

Blair sat up, took off the glasses. "Timothy, tell me straight and I'll let it go. I swear. Just tell me, is it dirty money? Are you into something I shouldn't know about?"

"Relax, Senator. I'm clean. I do honest work like skippering. I've put my time in as a deckhand. Worked my way up. I've got a pilot's license now. Up to sixty-five feet. In some circles, that's impressive. It's just that I insist on cash.

And I pay for what I need in cash. I don't owe anyone anything."

"I hope you make up some kind of credible story come tax time."

"No tax time for me."

"Don't kid yourself. I.R.S. has these monster computers that can match social security numbers with. . ."

Timothy shook his head. "No social security card. For a guy on the Finance Committee or whatever it is, you're a little slow at picking up this sort of thing. No credit cards, no loans, no social security, no investments, no bank. No paper trail. Unlike you, Senator, I'm strictly invisible."

"You ever figure what you've lost in interest?"

"You ever figured what you've given Uncle Sam over the years?"

Another long silence. "No one's ever asked you about your name? I mean, I may not have *voters* in Florida, but I assume some folks there watch the evening news."

"How old was I when I took off? Fifteen?"

"Sixteen. Right during a campaign."

"I remember that part. It seemed like you were getting a lot of use out of that name—all those posters and ads and stuff. High visibility, right? So I picked up a brand-new name. Just for myself."

"A different name? You can't do that."

"Went to court at eighteen. All legal."

"You've got no right. . . . So what is it?"

"I forgot."

"Come on, don't kid around."

"My mind's gone blank."

"Look, how do you think it feels, having a son and not even knowing his goddamned name? What is it?"

"Must be the sun," Timothy said. Taking off his cap, he fanned his brow in the darkness. "It fries my brain. Can't remember a thing."

In the silence, Blair could feel his pulse beat in his chest the way it did when he boxed at the gym. What do you do with a kid like this? "O.K.," he said at last, trying to sound jocular, offhand, amused, "how about an arm wrestle? One out of one. Sudden death. If you win, I won't mention this again. Be Timothy Khadafi for all I care. But if I win, you let me know who you are. And put in a phone so I can stay in touch. That's all. Just that."

Timothy shrugged and set his elbow down just as he did when he was a kid. Blair straightened his chair, drawing it up close, and placed his own elbow down carefully.

Suddenly Timothy's pressure was there. The first surge was so unexpected that Blair almost had to give in to it. But he recovered, forcing his son's arm upright again. Boxing and tennis had paid off. The two of them were locked in an even match. Blair could feel the tendons in his neck strain. As the pressure built, he imagined, crazily, an artery bursting, life's flood spurting. Gradually, half inch by half inch, Timothy was forcing his father back. It was impossible— the little kid. . .

"Good God!" Cleo's voice. "Are you two crazy?"

Blair felt a flicker of inattention in his opponent, and with a grunt slammed his son's arm hard on the metal top. Both glasses fell to the tile floor.

Blair threw himself back in his chair, grinning. "I won," he said over his shoulder to Cleo who was standing at the living-room door. His arm burned as if it had been broken, but he felt great. Turning back to Timothy he said, "So who are you?"

Timothy stood up, dressing with cool dignity. "That's something I learned from the way you played it with Mom," he said. "I don't keep promises unless I want to."

Astonished, Blair turned to Cleo. "I won, right?" But she, his only witness, had turned and left. And then so did his son. The boy simply vanished. In the silence, Blair shook his head. "I won, damn it, I won."

BALM STREET

The sound of bus stations, she decides, must be the same all over the country. Muzak muttering from the ceiling, garbled announcements in lo-fi, the snarl and wail of distant video games. Bert sits there trying to sort out sounds, wondering how many thousands of miles she has traveled on busses. Too many. She's ready to get back to New Mexico, back to the stillness of mountains. Is that a part of passing thirty?

There is another sound, a gentle mumbling. It's this girl sitting beside her talking to Bert about Jesus. The girl hasn't noticed that Bert's not listening. The girl's voice blends in with the Muzak and the video games. She is saying things like, "Love's a real high," and "Jesus really cares. He'll look out for you if you let him. He's like a pal, but he has powers."

"I know," Bert mutters at appropriate times. "Really." But her mind is elsewhere. She is staring out into open space, responding as she might to a child who insists on describing a long dream she's had— "yuh. . .uhhuh. . . right. . . really."

Bert is not thinking about Jesus one bit. She is thinking about Frederick who, though bearded, is no Jesus. He has been in the phone booth for a long time. Surely their friend O. D. Kraemer is either home or not home, can either put them up for the night or can't. She'd go over to the phone booth and rap on the glass and ask Frederick what gives except that it would mean lugging the duffel and she's low on energy.

"Hey," she says to the girl, "I've forgotten where this is."

"Cincinnati," the girl says. "Cincinnati, Ohio. But it doesn't make much difference, does it, because in His eyes. . ."

"Sure," Bert mutters. "Uh-huh."

"Excuse me, but like I get the feeling you're not really listening to me."

"I was sure we'd be out of Ohio by now."

"I mean, you keep nodding, but I don't hear Jesus in your voice."

Bert looks at this girl for the first time. She must be under twenty—a kid—and slight, the kind of build Bert used to envy when she was a tall, big-boned teenager. The girl wears the long skirt and flashes the quicky smile of all believers, living each day in joysville. Bert knows the pattern because she's been there herself. It wasn't this particular outfit, though. At Pacific House they were more Eastern than Western, more Buddhist than Christian. Jesus was wise but limited by his culture. The Buddha was The Way and would embrace the world as soon as the world came to The Buddha. The way was threefold—joy, harmony, and obedience. Bert recalls for the first time in years how her smile muscles ached after a day of outreach. She remembers how tired she got from talking to all those hardened, unsaved souls, all those stone walls.

"My name's Bert."

"I'm Clover." For just a minute the Jesus smile is replaced with Clover's own smile, but then it passes. "I know it seems like a real drag listening to some Jesus freak in a bus station, but that's only because when you don't have Him in your heart you have to stay on guard. You have to. I mean, when you're alone without Him it's scary and you need someone to protect you and guide you. But like He says, He has this big house with rooms for us all where He'll care for us and. . ."

"Got him," Frederick says. He's standing there in front of Bert, grinning like the green giant. "Took me five quarters. You're not going to believe what the hell he's doing."

"Joined the F.B.I.?"

"Funnier."

"C.I.A.?"

"Health spa."

"Works there?"

"Runs it. I mean several. Really."

"O.D.?" She can't imagine O.D. in anything but that cruddy T-shirt, can't imagine O.D. going mainstream.

"It's *Mister* Kraemer now. *Mister* Kraemer is not in his office this evening. . . . No, *Mister* Kraemer does not wish his home number to be given out. Perhaps he is at one of the other spas. Shall I have him paged?"

"Wrong Kraemer, I'll bet."

"No, I got him. I got him. We're meeting him at the place on Balm Street."

"Which is where?"

Frederick shrugs. He's not one for details.

"Hey Clover," she says, "you know Balm Street?"

"It's hard to explain. But I could show you. I mean, go with you."

Bert nods. "This is Clover," she says to Frederick. "She'll show us."

The two of them stand up. The girl is delicate and only as tall as Bert's shoulder. "Lead on," Frederick says. Clover smiles, goes limp, and slips to the floor, silent as a green leaf falling.

* * *

The trip to the American Holistic Health Spa and Nutrition Center was delayed an hour by Clover's collapse. It was a relief to discover that her only problem was starvation. They sat her on the stool at the cafeteria and kept her from slumping by standing on either side of her. To others she probably looked drunk. They paid no attention.

It was not easy to get food into her since she was on some kind of penance, but they started her out on a glass of milk and worked up to vanilla yogurt that released her like an alcoholic's first sip. With a little sigh she gave into the eating habit: a cheeseburger, French fries, fried onion rings, a chiliburger, and could she please have a side order of pickles? She topped it off with a chocolate sundae. After a rolling belch she assured Frederick she'd pay him back every cent and then some because he was a beautiful, beautiful person. *Oh boy*, Bert thought, where'd that Jesus go?

But now they are finally on Balm Street and Clover is their leader. All that junk food has done wonders for her spirit. There's a bounce to her step that, thanks to wooden clogs, makes her sound like a little pony. Jesus has been set aside for the present.

The spa is between an upscale cocktail lounge and an antique store. Two globe lights and a sign with gold lettering on black: "American Holistic Health Spa and Nutrition Center Inc." O.D. here? She can feel her pulse. After all these years?

Inside it's all Victorian—wicker chairs, mirrors with gilt frames, potted palms, and gas lights. The music is soft waltzes. "Funk-y," Bert mutters.

The woman at the desk is made up like a good-time girl from a grade-B Western—the young, dark-eyed one who was forced into the profession due to circumstances beyond her control. A reluctant sinner. *Sulky Sue*, Bert names her.

Sulky Sue ignores them as long as possible and finally says, "We're just about to close."

Frederick says that they're there to see O.D. and is told that *Mister* Kraemer is occupied at the moment but who should she say is waiting?

"Tell him Frederick's here."

"Frederick who?"

"Just Frederick."

She clears her husky voice and bends toward the intercom. Bert notices that there are no buttons on that silky white shirt. It's held together by faith alone. And no bra under that. Leaning at a calculated angle, Sulky Sue murmurs into the box that a Mister Frederick and associate are there to see him. *Some performance,* Bert thinks, shaking her head in admiration. The woman makes Bert feel like a lanky cowgirl.

The gravelly voice from the intercom is no more intelligible than announcements in the bus terminal, but it signals something to Sulky Sue who looks up at them with new respect.

"He'll be right out," she says. "Sorry, I didn't realize you were old friends."

"Wartime buddies," Frederick says.

Bert's the only one there to catch that one. O.D. and Frederick spent three winters together in Stockholm. Theirs was not a conventional war.

Actually Bert herself didn't know about Frederick being a resister until a few days ago. He'd never said much about what he did during the Vietnam period except that he stayed clear of the whole damn thing. Bert never asked *how* he'd stayed clear. They give each other plenty of space. That's how they get along. Space.

But when visiting his parents in New Jersey the whole bit came out. Lots of things come out when fathers and sons get together. On the bus heading back to New Mexico Frederick talked more about it, and they discovered they both knew O. D. Kraemer—she when O.D. was a super activist in Wisconsin and he after O.D. went AWOL and made it to Stockholm for the duration. Strange that it had never come up. No, she decides, not so strange. Frederick doesn't shove his life and beliefs at her. She doesn't even know whether Frederick *has* strong beliefs. Which is fine with her. She's had enough of those for a lifetime.

". . . three years," Frederick is saying to Sulky Sue. "We went through some rough times together."

"No kidding," Sue says, all of a sudden not so sulky.

"I wouldn't kid you," Frederick says. Bert looks at him quickly. Once in a while when he's working at Ski Valley he turns on this other voice that sends signals to women of all ages and types, and then he's astonished when they make moves on him. He's free to do this, of course; the two of them have no marital hold on each other. But it's not fun. It's the price she pays for the space he gives her. Only occasionally has she had to step in, define the limits. Those were god-awful, high risk times, but they'd survived—she with her pottery and he with his odd jobs here and there.

They really did better than most folks except when the money got low and he got lured over to Ski Valley.

Nothing heavy going on now, but he's got Sulky Sue aglow without even trying. She's giving him a long, poker faced stare sort of sideways which no doubt she's practiced in the mirror. What she needs, Bert decides, is a cigarette dangling from one side of her lips, but perhaps that's taboo in high-class health spa and nutrition center.

"Hey guys!" It's O. D. Kraemer. It's really him. Same old chunky, loudmouth self. Well, there's a bald spot now, and he's dressed up like a car salesman—wide-shouldered suit and open shirt. But it's really him.

O.D. flings his arms around Frederick, claps him on the back. O.D. is a lot shorter and heavier than Frederick. Why hadn't she remembered him that way? Maybe because O.D. is always in motion.

He turns and gives Bert a bear hug and a kiss. "How'd you two meet anyhow?" Before she can answer he's gripped both her shoulders and gives her a real kiss on the lips tongue to tongue, yet. *Brother*!

Frederick doesn't know that she used to do things like this with O.D. before he joined the Army. This and more. Some teacher O.D. was—a delinquent graduate student at Wisconsin, an activist, and what she now calls a womanizer. But she didn't call him that then. She was a believer in the cause and he was a leader, so she just did what she was told. He taught her all the arguments against the war, how to think, how to act. He even gave her the name *Bert* and made it stick. Liberated her from *Bertha* at last. It wasn't until later that she learned what true liberation was all about.

Now after all these years the wet and sloppy kiss is like the wrong photo slipping out of the album at the wrong time. Maybe she and Frederick should have stayed on at that cozy Greyhound station.

"Same old O.D.," she says, detaching herself, pulling her head back out of range. "This here is Clover."

O.D. squints at Clover and then Bert, doing some quick calculations. "Daughter?"

"Friend."

"Well hi there, Clover honey," O.D. says, not missing a beat. "You've got some real great pals here. Real great."

He sweeps them into a tour of the center: saunas, whirlpools, steam rooms, sun rooms, progressive resistance machines, a carpeted jogging track. It is almost closing time and there are only two patrons remaining, a solitary jogger and a fat weight lifter. They smile dutifully at O.D. who tells them they're doing fine—sounding like a drill sergeant on good behavior.

O.D. describes some of the equipment, but it's clear that he is much more interested in the philosophy—the holistic approach. Exercise is just one small part of what's going on here. He deals with the entire person, body and spirit. Members have to report every phase of their lives—what they are eating each day, what kind of work they do, who they sleep with, what they dream. . . .

Bert lets the pitch roll on, studying O.D. with the audio turned low, wondering how he got here from there. True, *there* is a long time ago now. Really none of her business what he does with his life. Still, she was what some people would call his lover and she never would have guessed all this. Never. He was such a tough, hard sonofabitch then, so damn uncompromising, always nipping and snarling at the peace people and insulting the liberals, driving them to the left. He had his following, though. And he was loyal to them as long as they did what they were told. A big *as-long-as*, she discovered. She was out on the street the day she refused to pick up a shipment of M-1 rifles.

She watches him showing off on the punching bag. Pow-pow-pow. His timing is perfect. Surprising since he was never into athletics. But then, he was always full of surprises. Like the night he told her he wasn't against the war at all. For him it was just another first-rate struggle for self-determination, and if the liberals and peace folks could be roped in, it was O.K. to use them. But peace was a middle-class pipe dream. What *he* was working for—this in one of those in-bed confidences—was building the con-

hope," he told her, pounding the mattress, "is annihilation. A goddamned clean sweep." It's no wonder she can hardly remember what he was like as a lover.

He's got Clover on some kind of bucking bicycle where she is supposed to peddle while the handlebars rise and fall, an awkward business in her long skirt and getting nasty now with the dial turned up to a gallop, making her head snap back and forth.

"For Chrissake," Bert says, cracking O.D.s wrist, breaking his hold on the controls and turning the machine off.

"Hey," O.D. says, grinning but furious, "where's that nice kid I used to know?" But she's got no time for him since Clover has her hands to her mouth and has to be moved real fast to the Ladies'. Once there, Bert holds her head and watches the junk food come up in surges.

She finally gets Clover back to normal and tries to soothe her. "That O.D. is a pig," she says. "He needs a good punch in the snout."

"Please don't say that," Clover says, her face all earnest and loving. "Violence won't save his soul."

Bert gives Clover a hug. "Oh shit," she murmurs.

When they emerge, the last of the patrons have left and O.D. has everything organized. The three of them are going back to O.D.'s apartment for the night and his old lady will make them a fancy Spanish omelet and, sure, there's plenty of room in his car for them all and that duffel too so let's get moving. His "old lady" turns out to be Sulky Sue and she apparently isn't being given a vote, so in minutes they are out on the deserted street corner waiting for O.D. to get the car out of the lot. Once again Bert has the feeling that it would be better if she and Frederick were back on the bus heading for New Mexico, but there is a momentum going that has a life of its own.

"He's still the organizer," Frederick says.

"You should see how he runs these three centers," Sue says. "He gets these customers really believing in what they're doing. They push themselves like slaves. They eat what they're told to and swear off booze or leave their husbands or whatever he says. They love it."

"I'll bet," Bert says.

O.D.'s car glides up and Bert laughs out loud. It's a gangster car. Long, black, with jump seats in the back and a bar. *A bar!*

"You are too much," she says, getting in.

"Knew you'd love it," he says.

Sue sits up front with O.D. Clover is perched on the jump seat facing back. Bert and Frederick have the back seat to themselves with an upholstered arm between them. Not bad after days and nights on busses. *Cinderella*, she thinks. Not bad. All of a sudden she's in no hurry to get back to New Mexico, back to the mountain cabin they share, back to stoking wood and toting water from the stream.

O.D.'s apartment is super modern. *Flash Gordon*, Bert thinks. Lucite furniture, glass table, white rug, and ugly paintings on the wall—a green nude, a bloodshot eye reproduced eight time. Bro-ther!

"Wow," Clover says. "You *live* here?"

"Knew you'd like it," O.D. says. "I can always spot a chick with good taste."

"Oh, I didn't say I liked it."

"'At-a-girl," Bert says.

"Everybody loves it," Sue says, and before anyone can contradict her she sweeps Clover into the kitchen, a space set off with cabinets below and hanging plants above. Bert can see the two of them through the leaves as if they had been relegated to some outbuilding.

". . . so which do you want?" O.D. is asking.

"Which what?"

Frederick laughs. "Don't ask him to go through it again."

But O.D. does anyway. It's a spiel about how booze destroys vitamins, burns them right up, so all he serves is good wines, the best, and some imported beers for the hard-hat set, and which does she want?

She shrugs. "Just so long as it's not sweet."

Frederick says he'll settle for a can of beer. "Aw, come

on," O.D. says. "I've got some really fancy vintage stuff here. Let me show off."

"Slow down," Frederick says, grinning. "It's going to take me a little time to get used to this." And to Bert, "Here's the guy who organized the militant wing of our colony in Stockholm, the Maoist minority, the cell within the cell. He even made the Swedes nervous."

"Me?" O.D. gives Frederick a look of injured innocence. She remembers that look. They even caught it in the newspaper once—the moment he was arrested in connection with the bombing of a laboratory. There it was on the front page: Would *I* do a thing like that?

"Yup. It was you all right. I went up there like most everyone else—just trying to keep clear of it all. But you and that little group of yours seemed to have all the answers. I was in no shape to figure out what was happening. No hard feelings, but you really had us marching lockstep."

O.D. smiles, shrugs, opens a bottle of German beer for Frederick, and pulls out a bottle of wine from a little refrigerator built into the bar. "Well," he says, wiping the top and then working the corkscrew in, "could be. That was two lifetimes ago. That was when politics was everything. I mean everything. I don't have to tell you."

Bert nods. She knows more about that than she really wants Frederick to know.

Frederick nods to be agreeable, but then he shakes his head. "I learned all the slogans, but I never was really into it."

"Bullshit, man. Anyone who took the Swedish express was into it up to his eyeballs. You weren't there on a health cure."

"Just staying clear."

"No such thing," O.D. says, his voice suddenly tough. "Just being on this planet puts you in a state of war. Those with us were a part of the solution; everyone else was a part of the problem. There's no neutrality in the people's struggle." He stops, cocks his head on one side as if listening to a tape recording. He looks at the wine bottle in one hand and the stemmed glass in the other. "Well," he says softly, pouring the wine, "that's what we always used to say, right?"

"We said a lot of things," Frederick mutters.

In the pause, they hear Clover and Sue laugh. What on earth have they in common, Bert wonders.

"What's the other lifetime?" she asks.

"What's what?"

"You said that was two lifetimes back."

"Ah, well, there was a pharmaceutical period."

"You?" Bert says, laughing. "In a little white uniform standing behind a counter. . . ?" She stops. It is clear from the way he is looking at her that he was not running a corner drug store. "Oh, no," she mutters.

"Oh yes." There is an awkward silence and O.D. raises his glass in a toast. Puzzled, Bert raises hers. "To faith," O.D. says, "that surpasseth understanding." Bert wonders if she is supposed to laugh. O.D. continues: "It made perfect sense at the time. I mean, coming back from Sweden with a new ID, even a new name for a while. And a new movement really rolling. You remember all that bit about freeing the mind, entering new dimensions? A grand cause. So I spread the word. Dealing, you might call it. A select group—top-grade stuff. At least at first. But like all good things, it grew. I'm cursed by success." He grins, shrugs, raises his voice. "It wasn't for the money, you know. I just stashed the green stuff in garbage bags. Didn't know what to do with it. I mean, I was helping folks get off the damn planet. Talk about space travel—hell, I was Captain Kirk." He laughs. Frederick and Bert do not.

"Kind of dangerous," Frederick says.

O.D.'s smile vanishes. "You'd better believe it. Three times I was one breath away from getting killed. A lot of real loonies in that group."

"Excuse me." Clover appears. How long has she been standing there? "Clarissa's been making all this egg and tomato stuff and she keeps thinking how good a bourbon and ginger would taste."

Clarissa, Bert thinks. What a weird name!

"She send you out?" O.D. asks.

"Oh no, she said not to. But it only seems right."

O.D. shakes his head, smiling. "*Not* right. She knows better than to ask. Like I said, hard liquor nullifies a whole cluster of nutriments. Talk about world hunger, this country is populated with starving people."

"Like where?" Frederick asks.

"All around you. Anyone who drinks booze lives in a twilight zone of malnutrition."

"Still the phrasemaker," Bert says.

"I'm not kidding. This is a sick country. I tell you, I'd rather be doing what I'm doing right now than anything even if it didn't pay me a lousy dollar. People come in these centers dying. Rich people. They're doing things to their systems you wouldn't believe. Mind-body pollution, I call it. Booze, junk food, pill popping, refusal to exercise. When they turn to me, they're desperate. And they know it. Once they sign up, I give them a new life. I have to charge them a lot or they wouldn't take me seriously. I pick them up by the scruff of the neck and shake their old life out of them. Diet, lifestyle, everything. There's no corner of their lives I don't know about. And they love me for it. We're opening two more centers next month, and I'll be coast to coast in another year."

"You mean Clarissa can't have a bourbon and ginger?"

O.D. stops and looks at Clover, incredulous. "Honey, the first thing you've got to do around here is listen to what I'm saying. I can't help you if you don't listen to what I'm saying."

* * *

After dinner Frederick and O.D. leave the dishes to the women and go off to a corner of the living room. There they sink deeply into nostalgia. There are old friends in Stockholm to recall, old enemies, factions that were in control, factions not in control, naive pacifists, solid Maoists, and punks who were an embarrassment to the movement.

Their talk walls them off from the others. They begin drinking beer seriously and munching pretzels and smoking cigars. *Cigars! Bro-ther*! Frederick never smokes except a little grass from time to time and O.D. sure doesn't sound like a smoker. How could they?

But no, it's not really them. Somehow they've turned themselves into war buddies, a veteran's club of two. They've converted that corner of the room into their club house in Stockholm, surrounding themselves with empty beer cans, cigar ash, pretzel crumbs, and old photographs. There's no reaching them. In that smoky haze they've slipped back over all those years and are comrades again, high on their shared misery, the two of them almost indistinguishable.

Clover has put her head down on the glass table top and is sleeping soundly. She has had seconds on omelet—consuming the portions the men forgot to eat. In addition she has had a peanut butter and marshmallow sandwich and a beer. She sleeps with the smile of the true Madonna. Bert carefully removes her long hair from the dirty plate.

Clarissa is in the kitchen cleaning up all by herself. Bert joins her, feeling sisterly. Clarissa's makeup has been washed off and reveals freckles. Bert is surprised at how young she must be—only a few years older than Clover.

"Stuck with the dishes?" Bert says.

"Nothing new. Besides, I'd rather do this than smell those stogies."

"Frederick never smokes."

"O.D. neither. Almost never. I've seen guys hustled out of here for lighting a cigarette. But those cigars are something special. Some old buddy smuggled them in. They're Castro cigars."

Surprisingly, the kitchen has no dishwasher. Clarissa washes and Bert dries. For a while they are silent. They work together easily.

Then Clarissa asks, "You were once his old lady?"

"You could say that."

"Figured."

"A long time ago." Pause. "It was kind of a hassle, living with him."

"I know where you're coming from. I sure do."

"Seems weird, thinking back."

Clarissa dumps the dishpan and wipes the counter carefully. "Not so weird. The guy's dynamite. When he's into something, he's really turned on. You know?"

"You have to put up with a lot of crap."

Clarissa shrugs, smiles. "So what else is new? I was a very mixed-up kid when I joined this outfit. He got me straightened out in no time. Gave me a new life. He even gave me a new name. I was born *Mildred.* Can you believe that?"

"He's big on naming. You know what he is really?" Clarissa shakes her head. "Oscar." They both laugh. "O.D. is his own invention."

"Holy Moses!" Clover's voice breaks in. "You know what time it is?" She stumbles into the kitchen, still groggy with sleep. "Like I was supposed to be back at the mission an hour ago."

"Maybe it's time you gave them up," Clarissa says gently.

"Are you kidding? Like I *live* with Jesus, you know. But I got to hurry. Oh boy, am I going to catch it." She gives Bert a quick hug. "Remember," she says, "Jesus is ready to take over your life any time you let him."

"I'll remember," Bert says.

Clover turns to Clarissa. "You're real beautiful all scrubbed like that," she says. And then in embarrassment, "You both are. I've never met people like you."

"You will," Bert says.

Clover goes to the door and shouts back to the men, thanking them for the food and everything, a little routine some parent must have taught her.

They hear her clatter on the stairs, wooden clogs making their pony sound, fading. Bert looks down from the window and sees this little kid hurrying along the dark, deserted street. There she goes, Bert thinks, rushing back to her Jesus. And she's going to catch it. Scrub floors, maybe. Fasting. Extra prayers. And she won't complain.

"Some chick," Clarissa says, still in the kitchen, wiping counters, polishing chrome. "I sure wouldn't want to go through that chapter again."

"Me neither." Or *yours*, Bert thinks, smiling.

There's a guffaw of laughter from the men in the other room and one of them calls out for another six-pack. With a jolt she realizes she can't tell which one spoke. The Frederick she's been living with is fading away in cigar smoke. A male voice calls out to hurry up for Chrissake.

Clarissa is already at the refrigerator, but Bert blocks her, shakes her head, goes in the other room.

"O.K., guys, let's not overdo the regression."

"Guess what?" Frederick says. "O.D. here has just offered me a job."

"I thought we were just passing through."

"Good money," Frederick says cheerfully. "And I'd be working for an old buddy. I tell you, this is a beautiful out-fit."

"No outfit is beautiful. Haven't you learned that? By definition, no outfit is beautiful."

"Hey kid," O.D. says, "why so uptight? Frederick needs something like this. Everyone does. I've even got a position for you."

"Prone, I'll bet."

"Jesus," Frederick says. "What's wrong with you? O.D.'s talking about a national movement, something really. . ."

"You feel hostile," O.D. tells her, accepting a beer from Clarissa. "Your stomach is in a knot. Right? Just join up and I'll have you turned around in no time."

"Uh-huh. Sure," Bert says. "Thanks a bunch, but I'm getting out of here right now." Did she really say that? With a jolt she realizes that this is one of those high-risk moments, but not like the others. It's not a woman this time. She turns to Frederick. "I'd like to keep on like we've been. I really would. But if this here is what you want, don't bother to write. O.K.?"

She picks up the duffel by the door and thunders down the stairs, biting her lip to keep from shouting to Frederick to hurry up, to get his ass out of there while he still can.

THINGS NOT EVERYONE CAN DO

The beachfront street of Venice, California is reserved for pedestrians. That includes roller skaters and skateboarders. Walkers are actually in a minority. They seem plodding compared with those who weave, turn, and spin on silent, lubricated wheels.

The sedentary and those temporarily in stasis sit in a number of outdoor cafes and watch the show. Even on that miscellaneous Tuesday morning during the off season there was a continuous stream, an unending performance for Dennis to watch. A few, he noticed, were beginners; but they were serious beginners. They didn't grab on to each other and shriek or giggle. Surrounded by experts, they worked hard to develop rapidly. The rest were astonishingly proficient, each with an individual style.

The roller skaters, he decided, were really more artful than the skateboarders. The roller skaters moved like dream dancers, some responding to silent melodies that came to them through their headphone radios. They swerved and twisted, turning backward, springing over curbs, dipping on one leg. They seemed to perform for no audience, but they passed and repassed the cafes, their Day-Glo blouses and shorts flashing in the sunlight.

Dennis Kepple was no skater himself. But he was no stranger to the scene either. He had lived in Venice for the twelve years since his graduation. Lived there off and on, that is. He was known locally as friendly but private, laidback but occasionally generous, a contributor to roller contests and street-art displays. He had a boyish, open face. People in the area trusted him.

Art dealers knew him differently. To them and to gallery owners on both coasts and abroad he was a rare and valuable phenomenon—one of the few artists in his mid-thirties who could more or less set his own prices. To fel-

low artists and to critics he was one of the four or five min-
imalists to watch. He had what the New York *Times*
described as "the ineffable chemistry of absolute contem-
poraneousness."

Until this week, Dennis Kepple had not been a cafe-sit-
ter in Venice. In fact, much of the time he was not in Venice
at all. His reputation was such that he was invited to show
in various major cities in the United States and abroad. He
also exhibited in small, provincial towns that, especially in
France, he had difficulty pronouncing. As for Japanese
cities—where he was particularly admired—pronunciation
was out of the question. But that was never a problem;
wherever he went, there was always someone assigned to
translate.

It seemed to him that he had been on the move continu-
ously for the past five or six years. His apartment was
empty more than it was occupied. It wasn't that he liked
travel that much, and he certainly wasn't a showman, but
the nature of his art required that he be present wherever his
work was shown. Indeed, he had to see the rooms they
would provide and see them empty before he knew for sure
how he would, as he put it, activate the space.

The phrase about activating the space was not actually
his. He had read it in an article about himself and liked it.
Dennis long ago adjusted to the fact that he was not verbally
skilled, particularly when it came to art. When forced to say
something about his own work he found it best to draw on
quotes or near-quotes from reviews he had read. It wasn't
that he wanted to fool anyone; it was just that those who
wrote seemed to have a gift for phrasing. That was their
area. What they wrote sounded more authentic than anything he could make up. Besides, using their words allowed
him to face interviews without stammering or suffering
from stomach aches. He liked to think of it as a kind of
recycling process—his gathering together phrases con-
structed in his honor and giving them back so that they
could be melted down and refashioned.

For the past two months, however, he had not granted an

interview or judged a show or left Venice. His withdrawal was noticed. "Apparently a period of intense introspection and regeneration," a critic in the L.A. *Times* reported. Maybe that's what it was.

Right now all he was sure of was that he was sipping beer and watching the roller skaters glide by, squinting in the glare from the beach and the sea beyond. True, he didn't normally drink any kind of liquor and he rarely had the time to sit in a cafe in Venice, California, but maybe this was what one did during a period of intense introspection and re-whatever it was.

What puzzled him was how knotted his stomach was. Like a clenched fist. For days. He rarely felt that, not even before major shows. The sun was warm, the air cool, the beer imported. He told his stomach it had no cause to clench.

Ah, there was Rosellen. A sight to sooth an ornery stomach. Rosellen was tall, thin, and black; one of the best skaters around. He knew her from the time she won the junior-high championship. And again the high-school award. Now she was two years out and doing what? He never saw her except on wheels.

She was a wonder at turns. With a single jump she would be traveling backward, arms out like a black swan. She didn't need a headphone radio; she made up her own rhythms. She always wore a plain white bandeau and diaper-like shorts hitched up high on each thigh.

She remembered him, all right. Everyone remembered him. But she never made a point of it. Never smiled, never nodded. Just the palm-down turn of the hand, the cool greeting. It would have bothered him except that she never offered anything more to anyone else. She was strictly a loner—no partners, no friends that he had seen. And always there. A real pro.

Gone now, with only that flip of the hand. Dennis told his stomach to relax. After all, what better salve was there than seeing Rosellen glide by?

Halfway through the next beer he recognized a blond

skater on the other side of the street. It was Kelty. She caught sight of him at the same instant, spun, stopped, hands raised in a pantomime of astonishment, then veered across the pavement, cutting off everyone in her route, right up to the hedge that defined the cafe, peering at him. "It *is you*, right?" she asked, still moving. He nodded, grinning.

She rolled around to the entrance, moving sideways now so as to weave between tourists, her head and left skate forward, right skate backward, looking to Dennis like an Egyptian goddess gliding across a tomb.

She wove her way past the hostess, swung deftly left and right around waiters, slalomed her way between tables, and dropped into the chair next to Dennis. She had none of Rosellen's liquid grace, but she had skill—the deceptive skill of a clown whose routines have been mastered with effort. Zipping nonstop from the other side of the street to the chair was a dazzling performance and Dennis was impressed.

"Absolutely freaked me out," she said, "seeing you sitting here like a ghost or something when I thought for sure you'd been hiding in Tokyo or New York or some such pitsville, so where the hell *have* you been?"

"Would you believe me if I said I've been to another galaxy for two months?"

Her mouth opened in wonder. Then her head cocked on one side. "You wouldn't put me on, would you?" She really wanted to know.

"Why aren't you chained to that desk?"

"Got the week off. Goldman closed the gallery—as you know."

He did know, now that he thought about it. She worked for the gallery that was about to put on his show. They had given him his very first show ten years ago, when he was twenty-five. "Fabric Suggestions," it was called. He had hung one handkerchief-sized piece of muslin on each wall and one in the center of each room. To his astonishment, either the show or the prestige of the gallery launched him. Rocketed him. Inexplicable, strangely unnerving. At college he had thought he was a poet, but that notion faded very quickly.

So now—ten years and a lifetime later—the gallery had begged him for another show. He'd been in better places in bigger cities, but he owed them a lot. So he gave them a show. Not a retrospective as they had requested ("A decade of spontaneous generation," Goldman had suggested), but all new. His stomach twisted up again. He wished Kelty had never come by to remind him.

"Tomorrow," she said. "I'll bet you can't wait."

"What's the alternative?"

"I can hardly wait."

"Try."

"Hey, you on a downer?" Then she noticed the beer. "You know, I read somewhere—*Art News* maybe—that you don't drink, don't smoke, don't snort. Freaked me out. So what's this?"

"Where do you buy stuff like this?" He fingered her vermilion Day-Glo blouse. The color set up shimmering vibrations with her chartreuse shorts. She liked strong colors—yellow hair pulled back, blood red lipstick, rouge applied with a heavy hand. And those eye-watering fabrics.

"Color Disco on Pacific Ave. You like it? You want it?" Her hands went up to the top button and he saw that, yes, she was really about to give it to him right there. People were forever giving him things.

"Just asking."

"I thought maybe you wanted to make something out of it. You know how you do. On a stick or a mop or something." He was squinting because behind her there was sunlight glaring off the beach and the sea, but she must have thought he was frowning. "Hey, I didn't mean that as a put-down. Really. I mean, I think your stuff is dynamite. Always. Every show. You never miss. Really."

"You want a beer or something?"

"Maybe a Perrier with a half lemon." He relayed that to a waiter. "There's this mystic guru in Seattle who lives on Perrier and half lemons for months at a time."

"Why Seattle?"

"His mother lives there."

"Figures."

"You don't have a mother, right?"

"How'd you know?"

"I read a lot."

"What else do you know?"

"No parents or family and no close friends and this is why your work has become a paradigm for the rootless anonymity of modern man."

"Hey Kelty, what's a *paradigm?*"

"Well, it's true, isn't it?"

"I think of it as distilling the ingredients of cultural vacuousness and presenting it as a potion to an unsuspecting public."

"Gee."

A muscular male skater flashed by, concentrating on speed. He wore silver pants and silver net shirt to match. His head was low, face serious. His only routine was moving from street level to sidewalk and back without breaking his speed or killing anyone. Not subtle, but impressive like a Bavarian bobsledder. He must have practiced for years. Dennis, watching, was astonished at a wave of envy that passed through him.

* * *

At two that morning he was alone in his apartment, unable to sleep. If this were another show in, say, Stockholm or Tokyo, he would be in the middle of assembling it. He would feel no tension whatever. Often he whistled. After that first year, it was clear that whatever he did would be a sensation.

Even the very first show was a lark, a kind of joke, campy good fun. Goldman had put him up to it, had made it all happen. One month Dennis was just a framer, handler, delivery boy his first job out of college; the next he was crowned "an audacious new talent, a minimalist who in one astonishing show has made his contemporaries seem con-

trived, and has outraged the general public in ways remind-
ful of the Armory Show."

If that was really what he had done, why not try it
again? The comic element began to fade as he began to sell.
There must be value to anything that paid that well; and
besides, the critics were utterly serious. Not one had a sense
of humor. If they'd been kidding, surely someone would
have laughed.

There were no rules he could see—except never repeating himself. From cloth squares he'd gone to paper. First
colored sheets—all the same shade of green—and then
notebook paper, the three-hole variety he used to buy at the
college bookstore. In Lyon he added a pencil line down the
middle of each sheet. He placed one sheet on each wall and
made sure they were all exactly 66-1/4 inches from the
floor. A London critic had written that the quarter inch
revealed "the subtlety of craftsmanship hidden at the very
epicenter of apparent capriciousness." Of course in France
they translated that quarter inch into meters or whatever, so
it didn't sound so special to him, but the French critics were
ecstatic.

Two in the morning was normally his best working
time. He insisted on having the key to the gallery and usually could put a show together in an hour or so, starting
from scratch. "The latent dream work," a Belgian critic told
him, "must have been generating for months." Dennis
agreed. Who was he to argue?

So this would have been his working time under normal
conditions. Something would have occurred to him on the
plane or at some reception. "What I need is a new wrinkle,"
he had said to himself in the cab from the airport to a
museum he couldn't pronounce in Osaka. And, sure
enough, a single crease on the upper left corner of each
sheet of wrapping paper gave the collection a dog-eared
look, "as if to suggest an irreverent, puckish questioning of
the eternal truths."

It was all going so well, he couldn't imagine why he had
taken such pains and such a risk with this new show. Two

months of effort—long days and many nights—working for
the first time in a rented studio. With clay. He hadn't used
clay since taking a sculpture course in college. Laborious,
frustrating, and a terrible mess. There were days when he
felt this was the most exciting thing he had done in his life,
but now that it was completed and assembled he wasn't sure
why he had done it. All those little human figures—how
could he explain it?

Strange that Goldman hadn't called before this. Not
like him at all. Was he angry at being told not to look at the
show in advance? Had it not generated the kind of advance
interest it should have? Dennis picked up the phone and
started punching Goldman's number. Needless, of course.
Goldman would assure him that the show would be a hit, his
voice as smooth as mineral oil. He would say they had
nothing to worry about. What was Kelty's phrase?—"You
never miss." True, but Dennis had to hear it from Goldman.
Two rings. Then: "Do you know what the hell time it is?"
Goldman's voice cold as a bullhorn. The Nobel Prize committee could have been calling, but Goldman didn't give a
damn.

"It's seven after two," Dennis said.

"Dennis, is that you? Something wrong? You must be
in serious trouble."

"You could say that."

"Don't play games at this hour. Dennis, what's wrong?
You stoned?"

"Just wondered if you'd seen the show."

"The show? You said no one was to go in there. Not
even the cleaning ladies. That's what you distinctly said."

"That's what I said."

"So why are you calling?"

"I just wondered."

"Preshow jitters? You? I thought you were immune.
Unfailing confidence. That's what I read in *Artweek*. 'The
naive certainty of a child prodigy.' So what's happened?
Just because you decided to start fooling around with clay
figures. . . ." Pause. Silence at both ends. Then, continu-

ing in a lower key, "Well, so I took a peek. Just a peek. From the door. I didn't spend time with it, you understand. Just a peek."

"Goldman, can I come over?"

"One drink. Just one drink's worth."

* * *

Goldman had the top floor of a commercial building overlooking the beach and the sea. It was a gallery of its own, a showplace. Dennis was pleased that one of his fabric constructions was hanging prominently and, yes, a yellow cone from his cone period.

"Scotch or bourbon?" Goldman asked.

"I don't really like either."

"I told you I'd give you one drink. I don't want you pacing up and down for the rest of the night. I've got things to do tomorrow even if you don't. We've got a press conference and a pre-pre-showing and then the regular pre and then the reception and oh Jesus you artists don't have the slightest idea what it is to run a gallery." He was mixing Dennis something, a lot from the bottle and not more than a splash of water and ice. "If you ask me, *we* should be getting the two-thirds for all the work we put into it compared with the fun and games you do. Except. . ." He handed Dennis the drink. "Except for *this* show, of course. This show. . ."

"This show is what?"

"Sit down."

"That bad?"

"Where'd you learn that word? You know that doesn't mean anything. Good-bad. Leave that to the clergy. Dennis, tell me, what the hell made you go off and do a thing like this?"

Dennis shrugged. He really wanted to say something, but the show hadn't been reviewed and he had no way to describe what he had done or why he had done it. "It took a lot of time and effort."

"You sound like a school kid." Goldman's voice was

low, gravelly—as if he'd been chewing glass. He walked up and down, sloshing the ice in his glass. "'It took a lot of time and effort, Sir.' Agh, you had it made, Dennis. First cloth, then paper. You hadn't even touched plastic yet. You were golden. Golden."

"Were?"

"Look, I'm not saying this is a *bad* show. You got that? There's no such thing as a *bad* show. What I'm saying is it's a *risky* show. Look. . . ." He pulled a hassock up in front of Dennis, their knees touching. "Think of it from the critic's point of view. Kepple is known in a certain way. He's known for being outrageous. Straight-faced, innocent looking, but outrageous. He's the standup comic who insults his audience. But everyone buys so they'll be included in the joke. You understand? To reject Kepple is to be a Philistine, a square, a clod. So they buy. And the critics say beautiful things. But now what? Now you decide to go representational. All those figures sitting there in their little boxes and tubs and what-all. I'm impressed. I didn't know you had any talent for that kind of thing. Must have taken you months to put something like that together. I'm really impressed. But never mind what I feel. What's a critic going to do with a show like that? You give him a choice of up or down and nothing between. One, Kepple has matured. But what does that say about your past work? And the work of your imitators? What about the galleries and the investors? These guys have sunk big bucks into your paper stuff. Is that now *immature?* These guys aren't in it for love, you know. Critics have a moral obligation to investors, right?" He stopped, sipped, shook his head. "So a lot of those critics will be tempted to swing the other way."

"Other way?"

"You know, something like 'Kepple's little statues are the all-too-familiar efforts of a second-year art student.'"

"Oh come on. They wouldn't. . ."

"You think? Listen, you've been walking on the water so long you've got no idea what sharks can do to you. I'm telling you, Dennis, they go for the tenderest parts first."

Dennis stood up and drank half the glass like medicine. "You're a great friend," he said, heading for the door. "Mr. Sunshine himself."

He was just about out of there when he felt Goldman's hand clamp onto his arm and spin him around.

"You don't think I'm the best friend you ever had? Listen, I've got every word every art critic has ever written about you. I've got every photo that's ever been taken of you. I can tell you the date of every one of your openings. Why do you think it tears me apart to think what they might do to you tomorrow? You want me to spell it out?"

Dennis stood there while Goldman embraced him. He could smell the Old Spice. He was startled but not shocked. He'd tried being close to men just as he'd tried the same with women, but both had made him uncomfortable. He knew that if he did not reciprocate, did not move a single muscle, that Goldman would let go, would quietly show him to the door.

* * *

At four that morning Dennis still had not been back to his apartment. He'd walked for what seemed like miles, his legs rubbery from Goldman's drink. It wasn't Goldman's affection that had left him shaken, it was his description of the alternatives ahead. Dennis knew perfectly well what critics and buyers could do to an artist. He'd heard plenty of disaster stories.

So why *had* he risked everything? All he had to go on were a clutter of feelings. For some reason it had felt good to give shape to clay, to put some of his own feelings into these figures, to do something that perhaps not everyone could do. But how could he put all that into words that would make sense to others? Perhaps if he were lucky some critic would phrase it right, would show him why something like this was important.

He could make out the horizon now, the slate gray of the

sky distinct from the silver streaks of the sea. He shivered. That shark image of Goldman's was decidedly unpleasant.

There was the sound of a roller skater on the street behind him. At this hour! He turned to see a single form moving fast. It suddenly leapt, turned, and almost fell. Starting up again, it went through the same cycle. It was, he could see now, a woman. Whatever she was practicing must have been difficult because she almost lost her balance every time. He thought of Rosellen—same build but too unsure.

She was not more than thirty feet from him on that deserted street when she tried the same routine once again. This time she truly fell—slamming against the pavement, lying there in a heap. For a fraction of a second he remained still, hoping she would rise, would go on with her practice. He had a high regard for privacy. But when she didn't move, he jumped and ran to her.

What should he do? He knew nothing whatever about how to help an injured person. She was face down, crumpled and indistinct. Dead?

No, she was shuddering. Silent sobbing, perhaps. Then she stopped and muttered an obscene word to herself over and over. That sounded fine to him. If she were angry, she'd be O.K.

"Let me help you up," he said.

She flipped around to a sitting position as if he had hit her. It was indeed Rosellen.

"Get your hands off."

"It's me, Dennis."

"What you doing out here?"

He lifted her up. She wore pads on her knees, elbows, and the outside of each hand. They'd kept her from ripping the skin, but the wind had been knocked out of her. He steered her to the park bench.

"I'll be O.K, in a minute," she said, sprawled there. "There's nothing broke. You ever try a double turn?"

"Are you kidding? I can't even stand on skates."

"Well, that's what I'm doing. Trying. Double turn."

"I've seen you do that a thousand times. You never miss."

"That's a *half* turn, stupid. Anybody can do a half turn. Kids do it. This is a double turn. First the leap, then two complete turns in air, and you land moving forward—on one skate. You have to do it fast. That's the trick, moving fast enough. Try it."

"I'd break my neck."

"Yuh, maybe. You read about the guy in Santa Barbara cracked his head trying this? Made him a loonie."

"Jesus, you'd better quit while you're still in one piece."

"Aw, it's worth it."

"What's worth it?"

She thought for a moment but no phrase came to her and she shrugged. "I don't know. It's just worth it. It just is."

She stood up, swaying unsteadily on her skates. "Hey, do me a favor. Don't watch while I practice. When I get it right, I'll do it daytime." She smiled for the first time. "I'll do it so beautiful you'll dream about it."

She was off down the street. He sat there for a moment, making a point of not looking, hearing the sound of her wheels fading, feeling the warmth and the confidence of that smile.

Then he headed back to his apartment where he slept soundly for the first time in days. He dreamed of Rosellen on her skates, doing what others could not, leaping and spinning, landing on one skate, arms out, moving with such skill as to make tears come to his eyes, her form flying with him like a spirit through gallery after gallery.